# Fence Busters

Each boy tried to force the game ball into the hands of the other.

Each boy tried to force the game ball into the hands
of the other.

# Fence Busters

## BY CLAIR BEE

GROSSET & DUNLAP   Publishers   New York

*To*

LITTLE CYNTHIA ANNE BEE
*Who so effectively employed a "full nelson"*
*on her father that this book never did*
*make the publisher's deadline*

# Contents

# Contents

# Fence Busters

# CHAPTER 1

# LOVE OF THE GAME

"AND that loads the bases! The ducks are on the pond and varsity coach Del Bennett has called time!"

Gee-Gee Gray, UNIBC's star sportscaster, turned away from the mike long enough to cast a friendly wink in the direction of Gil Mack who was seated a few feet away in the press box. Mack grinned back at Gray and kept right on pounding the keys of his typewriter.

"Three up and three on! Yep—State's freshman phenoms are off to a good start! Bennett's out there talking to Rickard now—stalling for a little time—hoping to cool off the kids—top of the first—no one out—no score.

"Yes, sir! The frosh are living up to all of Gil Mack's drum thumping so far. Gil's university press releases for the past three weeks have been exclusive—but exclusive —raves for this freshman team! Gil has tagged them with the monicker of Fence Busters. He might have something there! They haven't knocked any boards off the fence yet, but two hits and a walk is nearly par for the course! Bases loaded now and—"

Smack in back of home plate and in the center of a

1

group of students and older fans, a big, middle-aged man with a pleasant face was enthusiastically holding forth on the talents of the Fence Busters. Jim Collins was a baseball fan from way back and knew every kid on the field. And, as every old-timer in town could testify, Jim had been a real ballplayer in his day, a top-flight catcher. Any fan would have recognized the signs; the gnarled fingers of his right hand told the story. After his playing days, Collins had stuck right with the sport; teaching the game to youngsters; following the local high school and university teams; eating, sleeping, talking baseball. Indeed, most of University's residents felt that Jim Collins had given too much to the sport, woefully neglecting the big farm which had been in the family for generations and which he had inherited following the death of his father.

Collins was known all over the state. He had over three hundred schoolboys' names in the little black book he carried. They were the names of youngsters who possessed unusual ability and who might be interested in coming to State and learning a lot of baseball while they furthered their educations. Collins' all-absorbing interest was baseball. And second only to his enthusiasm for the diamond sport was his loyalty to the home-town school.

Jim Collins was a State University booster all the way. He made the rounds of the high schools and talked State to every kid who wore a pair of spikes. Not as an official of the university, but as a loyal booster. Cynthia Ann, Jim's only daughter, was a freshman at State, and the big fellow was as proud as punch that she was realizing the opportunities he had missed. Collins had dreamed of a son who would carry on his baseball prowess; a son who would star for State some day. But the dream had never come true. He had been blessed with a daughter who became the love of his life. Mrs. Collins died a year later, and "Cindy," Jim's nickname for Cynthia Ann, assumed the domestic responsibilities of the family.

Out on the diamond, in the on-deck circle, a burly youngster tossed two of the three bats he had been hefting toward the frosh dugout and sauntered slowly up to the first-base side of the plate.

"Who's this, Jim?" someone demanded. "Look at the size of him!"

"That's Cohen," Collins said quickly. "Played tackle on the frosh football team. Great hitter! First baseman. Played for Rockwell at Valley Falls. Hits 'em a mile!"

"Remember Man-Mountain Miller?" another voice chirped. "Looks just like him!"

"Nickname is Biggie," Collins advised. "Six-four and tips the scales at two-forty."

"Ice wagon!" someone snickered. "Looks like he weighs four-forty!"

"If he doesn't hit better than four-forty I'll buy you a new hat," Collins retorted.

State's varsity was a veteran outfit. League leaders the previous season, the champions had, at first, read Gil Mack's raves about Henry Rockwell's frosh team with tolerant amusement. But as the early spring practice weeks slipped away and word-of-mouth acclaim about the hitting prowess of the youngsters spread across the campus, the varsity stars became sensitive and began looking forward to the annual pre-season series as an opportunity to explode the myth. The lengthy and flowery articles which had splashed the sports pages concerning the diamond prowess of State's sensational frosh ball club had built up a burning resentment in the heart of every varsity player.

Coach Del Bennett was well aware of the feeling which had gripped his varsity squad. He knew that every player on the field was as tight as a drum with tension. That was the reason he had called time. And that was the reason he was joking with Hex Rickard and the infielders out there behind the mound. Bennett was talking about everything except the loaded bases. He was stalling for time, trying to loosen up his veterans. He laughed at his own joke, slapped Rickard on the back, and walked slowly back to the varsity dugout.

The varsity receiver chuckled derisively as he squatted behind the plate. "Just another hitter, Rick ol' boy," he chanted. "C'mon, knock him down! Better take your foot out of the water bucket, big boy! You're gonna get all wet!"

Biggie Cohen never blinked an eyelash; he stood there for all the world like another DiMaggio, feet spread in a wide stance, bat held high and steady.

Hex Rickard reared back and called on all of his tremendous speed to whip the ball down the alley across Cohen's knees.

"S-t-e-e-rike!"

"Wha'd I tell you, Rick, ol' boy! C'mon, get him out of here!"

Cohen twisted his spikes a bit more firmly in the clay, pulled his bat through in a practice swing, and waited quietly. Rickard stood back of the mound polishing the apple and watching the base runners. Speed Morris, dancing off second, kicked up a cloud of dust and yelled something unintelligible to the varsity chucker. Rickard toed the rubber and extended his arms above his head, watching the runner on third intently as he brought the ball down for the pause. Then he dealt what appeared to be another fast ball. But it was his famed knuckler.

The ball shot up in the air and then came in fast, twisting and bobbing toward the plate. There was a tense moment of silence and then a sharp crack as Biggie swung too hard, leveled a bit under the pitch, but got a big hunk of the ball. The blow brought a gasp from the crowd as the horsehide sailed up and up and up, high in the air. The ball seemed to hang up there a long while, as though it were looking things over, before it decided to drop lazily behind the right-center wall.

As the ball disappeared, the crowd roar crashed out of the stands and the frosh dugout erupted like a volcano as the team spilled out to greet the grand-slam hitter. Cohen touched all the bases and was mobbed at the plate.

In the grandstand, Jim Collins was pounding someone on the back and yelling, "Wha'd I tell you! Wha'd I tell you!"

Up in the broadcasting booth, Gee-Gee Gray had yelled, "There's a high fly floating out to right-center and that ball is going—going—gone! What a blow! What a blow! And he only got a piece of it!"

Gil Mack was waving his portable crazily in the air and yelling, "Fence Busters! Fence Busters! Fence Busters!"

And now, the mob of students and fans who had been fired with curiosity began to appreciate that there was something to all the talk about a feud between the freshman stars and the veteran diamond champions. The big turnout was unusual, to be sure, but this frosh team was unusual, too. The fans were still discussing Cohen's circuit blow when Belter Burke strolled up to the plate.

Burke changed the conversation by driving Rickard's

first pitch straight as a bullet all the way to the right-field fence. And that blow did bust the fence, the ball bounding sharply away before the sound of the splintered board had echoed back to the grandstand. Burke pulled up at second.

Butcher Durley followed with a hard single over shortstop and Burke was held at third. The fans were on their feet now, stomping and cheering. Then Murph Gillen, powerful frosh right fielder, lashed a vicious line drive down the third-base line, scoring Burke and sending Durley to third. Gillen pulled up at second. Nick Nickels, two-hundred-thirty-pound catcher, added to the pandemonium when he smashed the ball over first base. The clothesline drive kicked up the lime and bounded into the corner in right field. Durley and Gillen scored and Nickels held up at third. The noise of the crowd was one continuous roar as Flash Sparks, the frosh starting pitcher, advanced to the plate.

The grandstand fans listened eagerly now as Jim Collins extolled the virtues of the husky chucker. "Six feet, two hundred pounds, and all muscle," Collins shouted excitedly. "Every team in the big leagues had scouts camped on his doorstep last June!"

"Bet you were there," someone yelled derisively.

Collins beamed. "And how!" he called, nodding his head grimly. "Kids who get a chance to go to college shouldn't pass up the opportunity."

"Especially if they're big-league caliber and have a chance to go to State," the same loud voice interrupted.

The pointed remark brought a flush to Collins' face but he controlled the angry retort which sprang to his lips. "That's right," he said grimly, his lips clamped in a tight, straight line. "Especially to State! You know any other institution that's done more for people like you and me?"

There was no reply to that one. The university was a state service institution in the complete sense of the word, serving its citizens in every phase of the science of earning a livelihood; farm guidance and service, business administration, the sciences, medicine, law, engineering, and the all-important fields of education.

Flash Sparks had broad shoulders and big hands. He handled the long bat as though it was a toothpick. But he was too eager. He swung from his heels at every ball and went down on three straight throws. Hutch Kroll, the frosh lead-off hitter, sauntered up for his second time at bat in the inning. Kroll was a squat, bow-legged counterpart of the immortal Hans Wagner, Pittsburgh's great shortstop. He was a power-packed second baseman, a peppery holler guy. But Hex Rickard was bearing down now, and he sent his southpaw sliders blazing in and down around Kroll's knees for his second straight strike-out.

Speed Morris, the yearlings' shortstop sensation, caught Rickard's first pitch right on the nose, driving the ball right back up the alley. The ball was a flash of light, but Hex knocked it down and threw Speed out at first by a whisker to retire the side.

The freshmen got a tremendous hand when they charged out on the field and the big seven on the scoreboard seemed like a lot of runs. But State's upperclassmen were pretty fair country ballplayers, too. And they were plenty burned up by the events of the first inning. They pounced on Sparks' offerings with grim determination and got themselves five runs on four hits, two walks, and two errors. The bases were loaded when Biggie Cohen leaped high in the air to pull down a hard smash headed for short right field.

"Good hit, no field, Jim," someone in the grandstand chided.

"The Rock will take care of that," Collins retorted. "Won't have to teach that big first sacker much!"

There was no doubt about the hitting ability of the frosh. The innings which followed proved that. But their play in the field was a horse of a different color. The varsity couldn't match their power hitting but they took full advantage of every slip-up, every show of indecision, and made the yearlings "throw the ball." Perhaps "heave the ball" is the better term. Anyway, the fielding misplays of the frosh kept the varsity in the ball game.

There wasn't a zero on the scoreboard when the varsity came in for their last licks in the bottom of the ninth. And the score sounded more like football than baseball. The frosh were leading 29 to 28. During the hectic struggle, Henry Rockwell had called on three pitchers. Sparks had been yanked in the third and had been followed by Silent Joe Maxim. Lefty Byrnes had relieved Maxim in the eighth. Del Bennett had used four hurlers.

The fans were limp, hoarse-voiced and worn out. Collins was the lone exception. Jim was just as fresh and enthusiastic as he had been during the first pitch of the game.

"Byrnes will go to work now," Collins said confidently. "Now that the chips are down. He'll set 'em down one-two-three!"

"Better had," someone said. "If the kids start throwin' that ball around again, it will be all over."

"Byrnes is too temperamental to suit me," a loud voice proclaimed. "See that act he put on when Nickels let that wild pitch get away? Seems to think a lot of himself."

"A coupla big-league scouts seemed to think a lot of him," Collins countered. "They say the Eagles offered his ol' man twenty grand if the kid would sign."

"I heard it was fifty," a new voice added.

The fan with the loud voice snorted disgustedly. "Huh! Twenty grand, fifty grand, a hundred grand! What's it matter? A real ballplayer plays ball because he loves the game. This guy acts like he's doin' the game a favor."

"He's got everything," Collins said defensively. "Stands six-three, a hundred-ninety pounds, got lots of speed, a good change of pace, and a pretty good idea of where to put the ball. Anyway, when you're pitching with a gang of Fence Busters like this frosh bunch behind you—"

"You're right, Collins," another fan agreed. "This frosh team's the hittin'est bunch of kids I ever saw!" He pointed toward the left-field corner. "Say, Jim, how about that kid warming up out there? Know him?"

The fans in Collins' vicinity focused their attention on the tall, slender youngster who was throwing in the bull pen.

Collins laughed. "Know him? You mean *you* don't? I thought everybody in this town knew Chip Hilton!"

"So *that's* Chip Hilton! Wonder why he isn't playing? From what I hear he can do anything on a ball field."

"Don't know about baseball," someone said knowingly, "but it goes double for football. Kicks, passes, runs— Heck, he's the best quarterback in the country! Bar none!"

"Didn't do bad in basketball either," someone said significantly.

"Just broke all the scoring records in the book," Collins said lightly. "*In* addition to winning the national basket-shooting championship."

"Why isn't he playin' if he's so good?"

"That's what I've been trying to figure out," Collins replied. "Only thing I can figure is that Rockwell doesn't want to be criticized for pushing his own boys. Hilton pitched for the 'Rock' at Valley Falls. Cohen and Morris were on the same team."

"How about Schwartz and Smith?"

"They played too!"

"Looks like he brought the whole team with him."

"That's what I'm getting at—Rockwell doesn't want anyone to think he plays favorites."

"Game doesn't mean so awful much. Seems like they could all play a little. Oops, here we go! Varsity's got the big end of the stick up!"

The grandstand shadows reached to home plate when Byrnes toed the rubber for his first pitch and a strange stillness seemed to grip the fans. But only for a moment. Russ Merton, the varsity shortstop and lead-off man, fired the crowd once again as he drilled Byrnes' fast ball straight through the middle for a clean single. Byrnes made no play for the grounder, leaped nimbly aside, and watched the ball speed across second base and out to center field.

"See what I mean," the loud-voiced fan yelled. "See what I mean!"

Merton drove for second base but retreated to first when Bob Emery, the frosh center fielder, came in fast and fielded the grasscutter. That put the tying run on first. It didn't end there. The next hitter, executing the obvious, pushed a slow roller to the right of the mound and Byrnes fumbled the ball! Both runners were safe and that put the winning run on base. But that still wasn't all! Byrnes threw his glove disgustedly at the squirming horsehide and the alert runners promptly and gleefully advanced another base before Biggie Cohen retrieved the ball. That put Merton on third and the push-along hitter on second. Rockwell called time!

The varsity players, scenting the kill, were out in front of their dugout now, riding Byrnes for all they were worth. Rockwell and Cohen and Nickels surrounded the high-strung pitcher.

"Steady, Byrnes," Rockwell said gently. "Get a grip on yourself."

"I'm all right!" Byrnes shouted. "But where's the support?" He gestured toward shortstop. "Morris shoulda had Merton's grounder!"

"The ball went right through your legs," Cohen said softly.

Byrnes glared angrily at Cohen. "The bunt was *your* play," he snarled.

Cohen was astonished. "My play!" he echoed. "Why, it was right in front of you. I couldn't have fielded that ball if I'd been playing on top of the plate!"

"Stop it!" Rockwell said sharply. "The damage is done. How do you feel, Byrnes? Can you finish it out? Do you want to finish it out?"

"Finish it out?" the angry chucker growled. "Of course I want to finish it out!" He gestured toward Cohen. "That is, if I can get some help."

"All right. But if you don't feel up to it, say so. Hilton is ready!"

"Hilton!" Byrnes shouted, his face contorted with rage. "Hilton!" he repeated. "All I've heard since the first day of practice has been Hilton, Hilton, Hilton!"

# CHAPTER 2

## BULL-PEN FIREMAN

THE true baseball fan wants to see the game played up to the hilt, wants to see a player make a hard try for every ball and for every play. The fans knew the hot-headed chucker was solely responsible for the danger-ous situation and they resented his obvious efforts to shift the blame to Morris and Cohen. Byrnes, beside himself with rage, scarcely waited for Nickels' sign, threw too fast, and walked the third hitter. That loaded the bases and Rockwell again called time. While he was talking to the frustrated chucker, the fans began to boo and deride Byrnes and to second-guess Rockwell.

"Take him out!"

"Put in a real pitcher! Put in Hilton!"

"What you waitin' for, Rockwell? Rain?"

"Who's coaching the team, you or the bat boy?"

Rockwell's eyes flickered toward the bull pen but he decided against the impulse. The wily coach was trying to develop a pitcher, trying to help Byrnes find himself. The pre-season series victory was unimportant if the big left-hander could be taught self-control. He delayed as long as possible before heading for the dugout. As he turned away, he said softly, "All right, Byrnes, put out your own fire."

Byrnes was on fire himself. He was angry with his teammates, the fans, Rockwell, and the varsity hitters. He fired the ball directly at the batter's head. It was a fast pitch and only the swift slant of the speeding ball saved the hitter from disaster. But the blazing throw was too fast to evade the batter completely and careened off the cleanup hitter's shoulder. That brought an angry roar from the stands and sent the varsity charging for the mound. But the umpires and Rockwell and Bennett got there first and broke up the melee.

The damage was done. When the field cleared, the umpire waved the batter to first and Merton trotted across the plate with the tying run. The fat was in the fire. Last of the ninth, the score tied at 29, bases loaded, no one down, and the winning run on third.

Out in the bull pen, Chip Hilton and Soapy Smith had stopped throwing to watch the rhubarb. The two youngsters were lifelong buddies and formed an efficient battery. Hilton was a first-class hurler, solid in every respect. The tall, blond youngster had blinding speed, a wicked screw ball, a good curve, and unusual control of a deceptive knuckle ball. More important, he had poise, confidence, and self-control.

Chip's redheaded receiver was solid, too. Smith had square shoulders, a sturdy frame, and the freckle-face had a strong arm. Base runners took few liberties when Soapy was behind the plate.

"That ties it up," Soapy said disgustedly. "Now, I suppose the Rockhead will give *you* a chance. Hah!"

The redhead was right. Rockwell turned at that very moment and waved them in. Then the veteran coach turned back to Byrnes. "That's all, boy," he said gently. "I'm sorry you did that."

Byrnes mouthed a curse and threw his glove clear across the diamond. The angry gesture drew another roar of disapproval from the crowd, and a chorus of boos and jeers accompanied every step the disgruntled pitcher made in his progress to the dugout.

The walk from the bull pen to the mound is short or long, depending upon the situation and the traveler. Some baseball authorities contend that the good relief pitcher is a special kind of athlete; the kind of fellow who performs best when the odds are against his team and himself, who revels in the opportunity to wage the uphill fight. To such a "fireman" the journey is routine and the task at hand an old story.

Chip Hilton had plenty of confidence in his pitching ability and, like most athletes, preferred to be the underdog. But he was far from being at ease as Soapy and he trudged across the field. "I've got to do it," he was thinking. "Just got to!"

Behind Chip's worry about the game and the series was his fondest hope for a good start for his high school coach, Henry Rockwell. And the big goal, the prize which would make Rock solid with the State fans would be to win the pre-season series with the varsity and then win the Little Four championship. A. & M., Tech, Cathedral, and State were bitter baseball rivals and all were gunning for the title.

Chip wanted desperately to be a good college pitcher, to be a starter. He knew, too, that a fellow who had played for Rock in high school would have to be about twice as good as any of the other candidates. Chip grinned to himself. "This is a pretty good spot to prove you've got it," he murmured.

Soapy broke through his thoughts. "Fine thing! He waits until it's all over and then sends you in to take the lumps. Fine thing!"

"What makes you think it's all over?" Chip chided.

Soapy squirmed. "Er—well," he hedged, "I didn't really mean it was over. I just couldn't help wonderin' why he waited so long. Far's that's concerned, why couldn't he use Dean? Why put you on the spot?"

"Because Dean's a lefty. Isn't it good strategy to throw in a righty when hitters have been looking at a southpaw all through the game?"

"Yes, but why wait so long? Why, the crowd even got on him!"

Chip jabbed Soapy in the ribs. "Rock usually knows what he's doing, Soapy."

"I guess you're right, Chip," Soapy said uncertainly.

Speed Morris joined them at the shortstop position near the edge of the grass. "Tough assignment, chum," he said grimly. "But you can do it!"

Biggie Cohen was next, walking beside Chip toward the rubber. "Rough, real rough, Chipper," he said, slapping Chip on the back. "But you've pulled out of tougher spots. Just throw it in there! We'll back you up!"

Rockwell said nothing. He watched Chip begin his warm-up throws and then turned away. But the twisted smile which flashed across his lips was enough for Chip. Words weren't too important where these two were concerned. Each believed in action.

"Hilton now pitching for State Freshmen; Smith catching. Play ball!"

That was the signal for the varsity to begin on Chip where they had left off on Byrnes. They crowded out of the dugout and opened up.

"Fresh meat, Butch! Knock it down his throat!"

"C'mon, a bingle will do it!"

"Break it up, we're late for supper!"

Up in the grandstand, Jim Collins was really going to town. "You think Diston is good, eh? Well, you just focus your peepers on this kid. Best *I* ever saw! Watch him!"

Chip was facing third base, the ball cradled at his waist between glove and throwing hand. He pivoted quickly and blazed his fast ball around Harris' knees on the inside.

"S-t-e-e-rike!"

Butch Harris was a power hitter, and he took a full cut at every pitch, aimed for the fence. But Soapy called them just right, low and inside, high and inside, and low and outside. Harris went down swinging. Lee Carter tried too hard to be the hero. He forgot that a single was as good as a home run and popped-out to Biggie Cohen. That made it two away and the crowd abruptly reversed its stand, becoming suddenly aware that they were sitting in on a real sports drama. They realized that the big kid out on the mound conceivably might perform the impossible. And, just like that, they swung in line with Chip's teammates.

"Come on, Hilton, come on!"

"Atta baby! Mow 'em down!"

"Minnie" Minson took his time selecting the right bat, looked longingly at the left-field fence, and finally settled on a long thirty-eight-inch pole. Wrapping his big hands lovingly around the heavy bat down at the end, he stalked up to the third-base side of the plate. Minnie had decided to break up the ball game all by himself.

Chip came in with his blazing fast ball, a streak of white which caught the inside corner between the wrists and the letters. Minson carefully looked the called strike over and then stepped away from the plate. He took a lot of time before he got back up there, baiting Chip for all he was worth. Chip's change-up curve dropped low outside to even the count, and Minson again backed out of the box. Once more he used all the time possible before pounding the plate and getting set. Chip grinned, and when Minson was firmly dug in, stepped back off the rubber and off the mound.

That was the signal for the umpire to get into the act. He whipped off his mask and stepped out in front of the plate. "Time!" he shouted, slapping his cap across his thigh. "Now you listen to me! Both of you! Play ball and cut out this nonsense! Understand?" He stood there, glaring from Minson to Chip and back again, then replaced his mask and walked quickly behind Smith. "Play ball!"

Chip toed the rubber and waited for Minson to get set. Facing third and watching the dancing runner, he slowly brought the ball down to his waist. Holding it there the full second, he suddenly stepped toward third and sent a crossfire, lightning-fast screw ball around Minson's knees. It looked way outside and Minnie hesitated a trifle too long. Then, too late, he threshed his bat through with a mighty swing, fanning the breeze, and Chip was ahead one and two. Soapy called for a waste ball, then, and Chip responded with a wide, lazy curve which was high and outside.

Minson really dug in then and got set for the fireball. The pitch had all the earmarks, the same overhand swing and fast-ball motion. But it was Chip's old dependable, his control knuckler. The blooper came twisting and bobbing down across Minson's shoulders. Minnie had started his swing but checked it and recovered his balance. But when he saw the ball heading for the strike zone, he tried to knock it a mile. All he hit was the dirt, the force of his empty swing spinning him around and down, a second after Soapy had tossed the ball to the umpire.

The crowd roar started then, but Chip never heard the ovation. He was hustling toward the dugout, trying to escape from Biggie and Speed and Soapy who had him surrounded and were pounding him on the back and roughing him up as though he had won the game. Red Schwartz rushed out of the dugout and joined in the celebration.

Rockwell brought them back to realities. "Come on. Break it up! Let's have a hitter up there!"

Murph Gillen tossed away two of the three bats he had been swinging and advanced to the batter's box. Determination was written all over the face of the powerful hitter. Murph nearly fooled them on the first pitch, too. He dug in and faked a full swing before laying a slow roller down the third-base line. It was a beautiful bunt. But Minson made the perfect play, scooped up the ball with his throwing hand and, in the same motion, whipped an underhand strike to first to beat the runner by a whisker. The fans applauded both players. It was good baseball.

Nick Nickels didn't fool around. He put all of his two hundred and thirty pounds behind his swing and laid the fat part of the bat against a high, fast ball. The lofty fly carried clear to the center-field fence. But George Reed speared it, practically off the boards, for the second out.

Chip had been watching Dean warm up in the bull pen and expected Rockwell to send in a pinch hitter. But nothing happened and he walked up to the first-base side of the plate, accompanied by cheers from the fans and jeers from the varsity.

Ned Diston was the varsity's Number Two chucker, and he had been invincible the previous year with a record of six victories and no defeats. He had taken it easy with Gillen, but Nickels had scared him when the burly catcher walloped the high waste ball. Diston decided to bear down.

The first pitch came twisting in around Chip's wrists. It was a teaser. It looked fat coming in but broke at the last second. Chip started for it but checked his bat in time and stepped back.

"B-a-l-l."

"Widow" Wilder checked his return peg to Diston and whirled around to face the umpire. "What?" he screamed. "Ball?" He gestured with the ball. "You called that a ball?"

The varsity infielders came charging in, too. "Ball?" they echoed. "Ball?"

The plate umpire wearily doffed his mask and pointed toward the field. "Get back there and play ball," he shouted. He waved the objectors back toward the field and dusted off the plate, completely ignoring Wilder. The Widow might have been his shadow, yelling into the umpire's ear and shaking the ball in his face.

The fans loved it and got a big kick out of the argument, especially when the umpire straightened up, faced Wilder, and literally forced the big receiver away from the plate as they argued nose to nose. It was good fun and good strategy on Wilder's part. Wilder knew exactly what he was doing, knew all about Chip Hilton, knew him from high school days. He turned away from the umpire and started on Chip.

"You went through with the swing!" Widow shouted.

"Think you pulled a fast one, don't you? Wise guy, huh? A real smart cookie. Well, that's the last break you'll get." He gestured toward the umpire. "He won't let you get away with that again."

The umpire was in position now, mask adjusted, and at the end of his patience. "Play ball or else—"

Wilder played ball. He slowly pulled on his mask, squatted for the sign, and glanced up at Chip to note the effect of the argument. But he got little satisfaction. Chip was oblivious to Wilder's attention. He was concentrating on the pitcher out on the mound.

Diston shook off a sign and nodded for the next. He wanted to try his screw ball. The ball came in low and outside and caught the corner for the called strike. Chip never moved.

"Yah," Wilder jeered as he snapped the ball back to Diston. "Timid, eh? Lookin' for the free ticket, eh? Well, forget it, hero. We're strikin' you out!"

Diston shook Wilder off again and came in with the same pitch. And again Chip watched the ball go by.

"S-t-e-e-rike!"

Chip's inaction brought a roar of advice from the fans.

"C'mon, kid, swing!"

"Hit away, big boy. Nothing to lose!"

"Get that bat off your shoulder! Bang away!"

Chip waited outside the batter's box until Wilder whipped the ball back to Diston. Then he stooped for a bit of dust and rubbed the dry soil between both hands. Despite his efforts to the contrary, he found himself trying to figure the next pitch, attempting to outguess the chucker. Diston would waste one now . . . come in with something close just below the hands or down around the knees. "Then he'll come back with the screw ball," Chip muttered as he stepped up to the plate.

Wilder, squatting in the catcher's box, tossed a spray of dirt over his shoulder much to the disgust of the umpire. Then he looked up at Chip. "Got you talkin' to yourself, eh? Don't like it, do you? Don't like the responsibility, eh? Wait till we start levelin' off on you—"

"C'mon, play ball," the umpire growled. "And the next time, you watch where you're throwin' that dirt!"

The crowd cheers died away as Diston uncoiled and delivered. The ball looked fat all the way in but dipped at the plate to spin down around Chip's knees just missing the plate. All catchers are adept in covering the last-second flight of a ball at the plate and Wilder did just that, covered, and then edged glove and ball imperceptibly into the strike zone. And he didn't move; he just waited with glove and ball poised knee-high over the inside corner of the plate.

Chip backed up confidently, but he breathed a little sigh of relief when he heard the umpire's "W-a-a-a-h!"

That brought Diston and his teammates charging toward the umpire and Del Bennett leaping out of the varsity dugout. But it was no go, the umpire held his ground, supported by the fans. They wanted action and they were pulling for the blond hurler to complete the Merriwell finish in a blaze of glory.

Collins' grandstand crowd was kidding the big fellow and having themselves a time.

"What's he waitin' for, Jim?"

"Thought you said he could hit!"

"That pitch looked good to me!"

"Good? It was right in there!"

"He can hit," Collins asserted. "Just wait—"

# CHAPTER 3

## CHUCKER SLUGGER

CHIP was waiting for the screw ball. He watched Diston intently and was sure he had it figured correctly when the big righty shook off Wilder's first sign. "Here it comes," he breathed.

Diston's overarm pitch came in around the letters, but the ball didn't spin away. It came whirling up as big as a pineapple and then flashed in and down under Chip's wrists missing the plate by a foot. There wasn't any question about that one. It was way inside and brought the count to three and two.

Chip stepped back out of the batter's box completely disgusted with himself. How many times had Rock cautioned against trying to guess the pitch, to outguess the pitcher . . . "Sucker," Chip muttered. "Plain, ordinary sucker!"

Diston waited until Chip was set and then gave the apple all he had. The ball came whistling in and this time it was the screw ball, the varsity star's favorite pitch. It came streaking in with all the earmarks of a three-two fast one. Chip's eyes were focused on the ball, following its path right up to the plate. At the last second, it seemed, the fadeaway darted toward the outside corner.

Chip was a pull hitter, a switch hitter who pulled a ball from either side of the plate. Batting against Diston, a righty, Chip ordinarily would have pulled to right or right center. And his pivot toward first base would have enabled him to cut down on the running time. But this time he stepped toward the hot corner and put everything he had into a smooth, flowing swing, snapping his wrists through at the last second, and the crack was like a pistol shot. The power behind the blow carried Chip toward third base, but he pivoted quickly, regained his stride, and darted toward first in a desperate sprint. The dash carried him nearly to the bag before he realized that the ball had winged its way straight as a bullet for the left-field fence. Then he heard the crowd roar and fearfully turned his head to see the ball boring far over the left fielder's head and over the fence, a home run in any ball park! All Chip had to do was touch all the bases!

That wasn't quite all. There was still the little matter of retiring the varsity in the bottom of the tenth. One run wasn't much of an edge the way the upperclassmen had been belting the ball.

Chip had that in mind as he tagged each base. And, as he headed for home plate, he was thinking of one of Rockwell's hitting axioms: "Just meet the ball. Don't try to kill it!"

Chip could almost hear Rock saying, "The hitter who is always trying to knock the ball out of the park usually winds up watching the ball games from the dugout— watching the fellow who beat him out for a spot on the team hit the apple a mile just by *meeting* the ball."

Then Chip was mobbed at the plate and he forgot

all about outguessing the pitcher and trying to kill the ball. He was grinning happily when he ducked down into the dugout but he didn't forget to urge the gang to "go get some more runs." He flopped down on the bench and reached for his warm-up jacket. Then he heard the sneering voices, and he could scarcely believe his ears.

"Glamour Boy Hilton, that's what they call him!"

"Natch!"

"Must be nice to have the coach hold you for the hero spots."

Lefty Byrnes, Nick Nickels, and Belter Burke were sitting a few feet away, side by side, eyes fixed on the action out on the diamond. But their voices were cautiously lowered so as barely to reach Chip's ears.

Chip was caught flat-footed, shocked speechless, so unexpected was the attack. He glanced at Rockwell and his other teammates, but they had heard nothing. They were cheering Hutch Kroll, urging him to "keep it going!"

Chip carefully adjusted the jacket around his arms and shoulders, and tried to figure it out. Lefty Byrnes had received reams of publicity. And, so far as his frosh teammates were concerned, the big southpaw had gained a tremendous amount of respect because of the fabulous bonus big-league scouts had reputedly offered him to sign a contract. Chip knew little about Byrnes, except that the big chucker was driving a taxi at night to help pay his college expenses. But that was about all. Byrnes kept himself aloof from most of the frosh candidates. Nick Nickels and Belter Burke were the only exceptions. Chip had never seen Byrnes with any of the other frosh players, but he had noticed that Nickels and Burke seemed inordinately proud of their association with the famed chucker.

Nick Nickels had been a little on the surly side the few times he worked behind the plate when Chip had been on the mound. Chip figured his friendship with Soapy might have been the reason. Everyone was hustling to make the team, and Soapy had looked exceptionally good in the early workouts. Nickels handled his two hundred and thirty pounds almost as easily as Soapy Smith maneuvered his two hundred. But Nickels was superior with the stick. He powdered the ball and hit it a mile. There, the burly receiver's advantage ended. Soapy was a veritable workhorse. He hustled every second, chattered away a mile a minute, and kept the runners scared out of their wits by his clothesline pegs to the bases.

Belter Burke was another power hitter. The big left fielder knew how to get all of his one hundred and ninety pounds into the swing of a bat. Burke had seemed all right to Chip up to this point. It didn't make sense. . . .

"Don't get it," Chip was thinking. "I just don't get it!"

Right about then, Hutch Kroll caught a two-two fast ball on the nose. But Diston speared it, leaped high in the air to pull in the hard-tagged ball and retire the side. That sent the frosh charging out on the field determined to hold the one-run lead and the action temporarily shelved Chip's perplexity concerning Messrs. Byrnes, Nickels, and Burke.

The fans were fired to the boiling point by this time and they gave Chip another tremendous hand when he walked out to the mound. There was no doubt about the popularity of the blond bomber, the fans liked him. Jim Collins didn't have to sell this kid. He'd sold himself.

"Set 'em down, kid! Set 'em down!"

"One, two, three! One, two, three, kid! One, two, three!"

"Three up and three down, kid! That's the ticket!"

There were other reactions. Del Bennett, State's veteran coach, was a big-leaguer long past his prime. He knew baseball and he knew a big-league prospect when he saw one. Bennett was almost tempted to join in the applause. He liked the tall youngster. Liked the smooth windup, the graceful finish of his delivery, the way he rapped the ball and, most of all, he liked the kid's easygoing temperament. A chucker slugger with poise and self-control was something! His thoughts bounded back to the first time he had seen Chip Hilton. The boy and his crowd had been just one of hundreds who had come up to State on one of those high school invitations to visit and learn about the university's educational facilities.

Bennett's eyes followed the sweep of Chip's long arm and the flash of lightning which streaked from his hand to Soapy's glove. The kid had it all right! He'd earned it, too. He had dreamed of being a pitcher and had stuck to it. Hilton had been a first baseman on that visit, but he had maneuvered around until he got some college coaching on throwing a ball from the mound. Bennett grinned at the recollection. The kid's whole gang had been that way, full of spirit and determination. Del's grin faded. It was too bad all kids couldn't be like that bunch, that they couldn't play baseball up to the hilt and still be good sports about it.

Bennett's eyes shifted to Biggie Cohen on first base. This big boy was ready, too. Ready for varsity or for the big leagues so far as that was concerned. Del's old buddy, Stu Gardner, had been the first to tell him about Chip Hilton and Biggie Cohen. Stu had wanted to sign the kids for the big leagues when they were graduated from Valley Falls High, but had stepped aside when he learned that they were interested in a college education. Del Bennett heaved a deep sigh. "There ought to be more big-league scouts like Stu Gardner," he breathed.

"C'mon, Chipper, mow 'em down! Lay it in there, Chipper. We'll back you up!"

Speed Morris, at his shortstop position, was pounding his glove and kicking up the dust with his spikes. Bennett smiled appreciatively. That was the old spirit!

"Give it to me, Chipper, ol' kid! Gimme that apple! Right down the alley! Can't hit 'em if they can't see 'em!"

Soapy Smith's chanting drew Bennett's eyes. He remembered Smith, all right. How could anyone forget the redheaded, freckle-faced comedian. Especially when he pulled that big wide smile which set his red freckles dancing.

Soapy's peg to second after Chip's last warm-up throw brought Bennett back to the business at hand. He turned toward Widow Wilder, who was waiting patiently at the bat rack. "Okay, Wilder," he said sharply, "work him! You get on and we'll push you around. I'm sending Rip King in to pinch-hit for Diston. Len Harris is warming up in the bull pen. C'mon, now, we've got to get a run!"

Widow Wilder was a real gabby guy behind the plate. The husky receiver ostensibly talked to his chucker but his remarks were always directed to the batter, obvious attempts to "get the hitter's goat." But Wilder could take lessons from Soapy Smith. He had never been exposed to a line like Soapy's. Soapy started right in and reversed the big catcher's own tactics. The redhead had writhed in anger when Wilder had been baiting Chip. Anyone who opposed Chip Hilton was Public Enemy Number One in Soapy's book.

"Chip! Look who's here! The black widow herself! And no skirts!"

"Aw, Chip, let's be gentlemen! Throw underhand! You know, women and children first and all that stuff."

Soapy squatted and gave the sign. Then, before Chip had time to toe the rubber, Soapy stepped across the plate in front of Wilder. "Excuse me, Miss er—Miss er— Oh, well, just skip it!" He turned to the umpire. "Excuse me, sir, do you have a soft ball?"

The umpire glared angrily at Soapy. Then, without a word, he lifted the sleeve of his blue coat, and watching his wrist watch, began to count the seconds. That did it! Soapy rushed back to his position with exaggerated haste and Chip slipped a fast ball across the plate for a called strike. Wilder was boiling with rage and eyed Soapy with murder in his eyes. His grasp on the bat was so tight he couldn't have hit a basketball.

Soapy ignored Wilder's angry glare and resumed his conversation with Chip. "Tut-tut, Chipper. That wasn't nice. Remember—remember how they let you hit the home run! C'mon, now, be a gentleman."

Chip wanted to strike Wilder out as much as he had ever wanted to set anyone down. So he shook Soapy off until he got the pitch he wanted. Then he drifted a wide, sweeping curve to the outside corner, and Wilder missed it by a foot. Soapy held the ball in front of Wilder and turned it slowly in his hand. "This is it, Widow. This little round thing."

Chip and Soapy had the right idea on the next pitch —something close in around Wilder's wrists. The screw ball did the trick. It looked as if it was going to split the plate but sliced in and down under the angry catcher's elbows and he never had a chance. Wilder had started his swing and couldn't stop and the umpire called him out. Strangely enough, the Widow made no protest. He glared at the umpire and then gave Soapy a long look and stalked back to the varsity dugout. Soapy loved it!

Chip's infield teammates were certainly giving him vocal support. They were chattering away for all they were worth: "Atta baby, Chip, ol' kid!" "That's the big one, Chip! Let me have number two!" "Bear down, big boy!" "Let 'em hit! We'll back you up!" "Mow 'em down, Chip, send 'em home!"

The infield chatter was great, but few if any observers noticed the absolute absence of outfield support. Belter Burke in left, Bob Emery in center, and Murph Gillen in right, were leaning forward, hands on knees, absolutely silent.

In the dugout, watching Chip with smoldering eyes, Lefty Byrnes and Nick Nickels were half-hoping the varsity would knock him out of the box. Yet, if someone had quizzed these five boys to determine the reason for their stand, he would probably have ended up completely in the dark. They couldn't have given a single logical reason for their dislike for Chip Hilton.

A psychologist might have been able to read between the lines and locate the trouble. That is, if he could have talked to each of the five players. In the end, he would have concentrated on Lefty Byrnes and come up with the simple diagnosis that the star chucker had been bitten by the "green-eyed monster" and had used his influence to poison the minds of his friends and admirers. Byrnes had turned his group against Chip because of his jealousy.

Gil Mack had played up Chip's all-around athletic ability several times and once had written a special story about the Valley Falls star which had been featured in the Sunday magazine section of the *Herald*.

In every group and on every team, challengers emerge seeking the leadership. Chip Hilton possessed the right qualities. He was personable, modest, sufficiently aggressive, was a fine athlete, had a quiet confidence in his ability to meet each situation as it came, and he was a gentleman. He was a natural.

Lefty Byrnes had all the physical qualities but he had been spoiled by too much praise and adulation. Fame had come too early and he believed everything he read about himself. Some athletes can read their press clippings and forget all the adjectives. Byrnes wasn't the type. The big portsider was afflicted with a difficulty which often attacks youngsters with too much ego. Knute Rockne, Notre Dame's immortal football coach, used to describe the affliction as "a swelling of the occipital bones."

Chip tried to put the dugout experience out of his thoughts as the next hitter advanced to the plate. He had expected Del Bennett to send in a pinch hitter for Diston and he measured his next opponent carefully.

Rip King stood about five-nine and was built like a block of granite. Chip had never seen the pinch-hitting outfielder before but he realized that the fellow had all the earmarks of a natural hitter. King walked confidently up to the first-base side of the plate and dug in at the back of the batter's box. He poised his bat steadily over his shoulder and fixed Chip with keen, steady eyes.

Soapy had measured the hitter, too. And, like Chip, Soapy figured that here was a real hitter. Soapy squatted and tentatively gave Chip the sign for a fast ball. Chip promptly shook him off, sensing that King liked the fast ones. Soapy then called for a hook and Chip settled for that, sending in a sharp, darting curve around King's wrists. It was close, but the umpire called it a ball. Chip came right back with the same pitch and again the arbiter called, "Waah!" So Chip was behind in the count and the varsity players really opened up and got on him with all sorts of suggestions and advice.

Chip sized up King again and once more decided against the fast ball. He passed up the blooper, too, and settled for the screw ball. The pitch came in fast toward King's wrists and then split the plate, knee-high. Rip waited that one out and the count was two and one. Chip kept shaking off Soapy's signs until the call was for the blooper. He faked his fast ball and sent the high-looping knuckler in toward the strike zone. It seemed almost as if King was waiting for the pitch because he made no false motion, simply waited until the ball dropped into hitting distance and then leveled off. There was a sharp crack and King golfed the ball high in the air toward the short right-field fence.

Murph Gillen had started in fast but reversed his field when he saw the ball was hit harder than it appeared. It should have been an easy out, but the bad start was too much of a handicap and the ball dropped behind Gillen and rolled to the fence. King skipped around first and held up at second, and the tying run was in scoring position.

Russ Merton was an ideal lead-off man. The five-seven shortstop crowded the plate, had a good eye, and was a consistent .300 hitter. Chip got the count to two and two, and then Merton topped the ball, sending it weakly along the third-base line. Kroll came up with it all right but threw wildly to first, pulling Cohen off the bag. Biggie was lucky to stop the ball, but he scooped it up and pegged it right back to third base where Morris was covering. It was a perfect clothesline throw and had King by a mile, but Speed dropped the ball. Rip King gleefully slid into the base, and Russ Merton scampered safely down to second. The winning run was on second base and the varsity was tearing down the dugout.

In the frosh dugout, Nick Nickels lowered his head and grinned when Lefty Byrnes nudged him with his elbow. "Here he goes," Nick said softly.

"Doesn't make me mad," Byrnes whispered.

Jim Collins' grandstand gang was all in a dither. There wasn't one of the fans who wasn't pulling for the frosh, but they had to voice their opinions. Baseball rooters are like that!

"Same old thing," someone remarked. "Good hit, no field!"

"Frank Merriwell doesn't seem to be doin' so good!"

Jim Collins turned to face the speaker. "You can't blame Hilton for the errors," he said defensively. "Heck, he can't do everything!"

"They hit the ball, didn't they?"

Collins shrugged. "If you call that hitting the ball you don't know much baseball."

Chip served four straight balls. Soapy stepped out of the catcher's box each time to catch the wide pitches. Chip was purposely loading the bases, giving the varsity push-along hitter, Tubby Ryder, an intentional pass, setting up a play at any base.

A grandstand heckler nudged a seatmate and directed a remark toward Jim Collins. "If this Hilton is so good," he said derisively, "let's see him scramble out of this hole!"

# CHAPTER 4

## GRANDSTAND PLAY

INSIDE baseball always intrigues the baseball fan. And vital game decisions provide him with wonderful opportunities to second-guess the big-league manager or the college coach. Critical game situations, demanding snap-judgment decision, develop in sand-lot choose-up games as often as they do in big-league parks. That is one of the many reasons baseball is the national game.

The situation which developed in the last frame of the hectic contest between State's varsity and freshman teams was exactly what the fans would have ordered: "Bottom of the tenth, the varsity at bat, one run behind, one down, bases loaded!" The opinions in the grandstand and in the bleachers flew fast and furious.

"It's a tough spot!"

"And how! Especially with the Number Three hitter up, and the cleanup slugger on deck!"

"They'll hit away!"

"Uh, uh, it will be the squeeze."

"Bentley and Reed are good hitters. One of the two will hit the ball. That's for sure!"

"Could be! But s'pose Bentley hits the ball on the

ground and into a double play? The game will be over and Del Bennett will get the blame for losing the game."

"So what! He gets paid, doesn't he?"

"What's that got to do with it? He wants to win!"

"Who doesn't?"

"Well, then, he'll squeeze in the tying run. And if Bentley is thrown out at first, so what? The game will be tied up and Reed can win the game with any kind of a hit."

"Sounds good."

Standing back of the mound, glove under his arm, Chip was polishing the ball between his bare hands. But he was doing something else, he was doing some tall thinking. According to his lights, it had to be the squeeze. At that moment, Rockwell called time and joined Chip and Soapy and the entire infield. The players waited quietly for Rock's decision.

"Their only play is the bunt," Rockwell said decisively. "Bennett will play safe and play for the tying run. We'll move in and stop the play at the plate! O.K.?"

"Right," Biggie said quickly. "Right!"

"It's up to you, gang," Rockwell said gently. "Make 'em earn it!"

Bentley made a great show of digging in, squirming his spikes in the ground and swishing his bat through in a full swing. But the act meant nothing to Chip and the frosh infielders; they were playing for the bunt even if Bentley knocked the ball down their collective throats.

Chip came in with a high, fast one and Bentley never moved. He had evidently been told to "take one."

"B-a-l-l!"

Chip decided right then that he'd slip the next one into the strike zone. He wasn't going to get too far behind.

The varsity players were out in front of their dugout and greeted the umpire's call with a boisterous cheer. They followed that with a barrage of catcalls and hoots for Chip, and a lot of advice for Bentley.

"Make him pitch, Bill! A walk is as good as a hit!"

"Wait him out, Billy boy! You got him worried."

"Here you go, freshman! Showers for you!"

Chip heard them. A fellow out on the mound doesn't do any chattering, but he hears a lot; hears his teammates and the opposing players and the crowd noise, and especially the fellow with the foghorn voice who never misses any game, it seems. The chucker hears a lot until he goes into his motion and concentrates on the strike zone.

Chip knew Bentley wasn't going to go for a bad one. A walk *was* as good as a hit. . . . As good? Better! Well, Chip Hilton wasn't going to issue a pass right now . . .

Soapy called for a hook and Chip came in with a low curve which caught the outside corner around the knees. The umpire's right hand shot up in the air and that evened the count at one and one. Chip felt better.

Rip King was dancing away from third, and Tubby Ryder was scuffing up the dirt close to first; but neither strayed very far. They were playing it safe. Not so Russ Merton. Merton was taking a big lead, practically daring Chip to trap him between second and third. Soapy called for the fast one and Chip nodded.

Toeing the rubber and facing third, Chip glanced toward the plate for Soapy's target. It took all his self-control to still the start of surprise when Soapy flashed the sign for the pick-off play. Cold sweat broke from Chip's forehead. He had nearly moved, might have committed a balk. . . .

Chip counted three and turned his head slowly from

third to second. Yes, Speed had caught Soapy's sign and darted behind Merton. The throw would have nailed the stocky little shortstop by a mile if the wily little veteran had tried to get back to the bag.

But Merton hadn't even moved when Morris sprinted for the sack. Russ would have kept going toward third to draw the throw, and King would have dashed for home. That would have meant at least two and maybe three pegs, and the way the gang had been throwing the ball around, anything might happen. . . . No, he wasn't going to risk it. . . . But he felt a twinge of regret when he noted the hurt expression on Soapy's face and the surprised look Speed flashed in his direction.

Chip shook his head regretfully and then put everything he had into his speed ball. The runners broke with the delivery, King leading the way. The squeeze was on!

It was beautiful to watch, if one was a spectator. Bentley whirled and leveled his bat in the bunt position and, at the same time, Chip, Biggie, Durley, Morris, and Kroll sprinted forward as if pulled by the same string. The ball flashed straight for the center of the strike zone, shoulder-high, and Bentley plopped a perfect spinner in fair territory six feet to the left of the plate.

Chip was a step ahead of King, dashing for the whirling ball. One agonized glance told him that Soapy could never make the play, and Durley was too far behind the runner. Soapy couldn't reach the ball, but he leaped forward and crouched in front of the plate. Bentley would sure have to bowl Soapy over to score that run.

It looked like a certain tally and the varsity exploded

with a mighty cheer. Then Chip made his move, dove for the ball just as King started his slide. Chip hurtled through the air just as if he was executing a diving roll block on the football field.

What happened thereafter was difficult to follow. Chip's spinning body tumbled into King and the two flying bodies sprawled in a tangle of legs and arms in front of the plate. But the ball was in Chip's hand and the precious sphere was pressed tightly against King's left ankle.

Soapy leaped aside at the last instant and the umpire took his place. Standing astride the plate, the arbiter caught the full force of the plunging bodies and was cut down as if by a scythe. But his right hand was held high in the air with the thumb pointing over his shoulder and that gesture brought a tremendous roar from the crowd. The runner was out!

Chip tossed the ball to Soapy and called time. When he scrambled to his feet a terrific burst of applause broke from the stands. And the fans kept it up, cheering and stomping their feet in a continuous thunder of approval. Jim Collins was jumping up and down like a little boy and yelling at the top of his voice, and the expert with the aggressive antipathy toward Lefty Byrnes was still at it, still making comparisons. "See the difference between this here Hilton and that Lefty Byrnes!" he shouted. "See what I mean? See? You see?"

Lefty Byrnes and Nick Nickels had leaped to their feet and were leaning over the apron of the dugout to watch the action. Byrnes was green with envy. "Grandstand play," he sneered. "Grandstander!"

"It was a neat play," Nickels said grudgingly. "Don't know how he did it!"

Rockwell rushed out on the field and pushed through

the circle of players who surrounded Chip. He clamped Chip's arm. "You all right, Chipper?" he asked anxiously. "You sure you're all right?"

Chip grinned and nodded. "Sure," he said lightly. "Sure I'm all right."

Biggie Cohen laughed. "All right?" he repeated. "All right? I'll say he is!"

Rip King was pretty badly shaken up, but he patted Chip on the back before he turned for the varsity dugout. "Nice going, fellow," he said ruefully. "I didn't even see you coming."

Del Bennett was halfway to the plate to launch a protest but King's action made him change his mind. "What a play," he muttered admiringly.

The stands were still buzzing when the plate umpire called "play ball" and Chip faced the plate. It was two away, now, and the frosh infield was playing deep, ready for a play at any base for the third out—and the victory! Not that they felt the game was in the bag. No, they had too much respect for George Reed. The varsity cleanup hitter had four for four so far in the game. No, this game wasn't in the bag by a long shot. The varsity wasn't throwing in the towel with the bases loaded and a hitter like Reed at bat.

Reed was a big fellow who batted righty and carried his bat high. Chip kept the ball low and inside. The big center fielder passed up three and then fouled three straight. So, it was the three-two pitch, and the runners moved with Chip's delivery. It was another screw ball around the knees and Reed hit it.

This time the ball was fair, a white streak which the fans never saw. But they did hear two loud cracks, two rifle shots, it seemed. And they saw Chip Hilton spin clear around with extended glove and keep on turning and run toward the frosh dugout. On the way, they saw him toss the ball to his coach, Henry Rockwell.

After that, they saw the umpire's arm extended over his head with the thumb pointing over his shoulder and they knew the game was over. Then they realized that the blond chucker must have snared a ball that was hit so hard they never even saw it leave the bat. And they knew, too, that the freshmen had won the first game of the pre-season series from the varsity. A bunch of kids had beaten the conference champions.

Gee-Gee Gray was talking into the mike at the rate of a mile a minute. Gray had caught Gil Mack's fire and was as enthused about the Fence Busters as the university press expert.

"—never saw the ball—but I know Hilton caught it, because the force of the ball whirled him clear around and he kept right on toward the dugout with the ball in his glove.

"It was a great catch—but the play—*the* play was the second out—the play at the plate.

"That play, fans, was one of the greatest this reporter has ever had the privilege to witness. Chip Hilton, the frosh pitching and hitting sensation of this game, to say the least, dove for the ball—picked it up as he turned in the air—and then crashed into King with a perfect roll block—knocked Rip's foot way from the plate— *and* tagged him with the ball while he was spinning through the air.

"If I live to be a thousand I won't see that play duplicated. This kid is sensational. I've seen hundreds of sensational plays during the years I've been bringing you State sports but—the thriller of a lifetime—that play was it. And I mean it!

"This kid—this Chip Hilton—has already established

himself in my book as the greatest athlete ever to matriculate at the university. And, unless I miss my guess, I'll have lots of company. I've got lots of company right now. Listen to the hand the kid is getting.

"Just in case you're wondering why there's a S.R.O. crowd here today—let me explain. This freshman team is the most publicized sports outfit ever to represent the university.

"State students and University residents are wild about football and everyone in this part of the state contracts backboard fever during the hardcourt season. But baseball is the game that holds the fans the year-round—the hot-stove debates—the grapefruit games—the regular season—the World Series—yep—baseball is the year-round pastime. And there are no more loyal baseball fans in the world than those right here in University.

"To get back to the reason for the big crowd gathered here to see this first game of State's pre-season series.

"The varsity is a veteran team and conference champs, but the kids—the Fence Busters—have stolen the show—gotten all the publicity—caught the fancy of the fans—and the varsity doesn't like it.

"Yes, sir, Babe Ruth made baseball history because he was a slugger. These kids are sluggers too—they proved that today. And they also proved that all the advance publicity about their hitting ability was *not* goulash. The varsity don't like all that whipped cream for the newcomers on State's sports scene, and quite a feud has developed. This afternoon the kids have added insult to injury by slugging through a thrill-packed game to take the lead in the series.

"You better get out here early Friday afternoon. Now for the statistics on the game—"

The crowd had swarmed out on the diamond, and as they moved slowly toward the parking lots and the gym, the name of Chip Hilton was on the lips of every fan. Jim Collins had picked up some new listeners and was telling them all about Chip Hilton and the Fence Busters.

Lefty Byrnes and Nick Nickels trudged silently along with the crowd in the direction of the gym. Ahead they could see a swarm of fans and players packed solidly around Chip, trying to pat him on the back, still showering him with their praises.

Emery, Burke, and Gillen waited by the gate and the three outfielders fell in beside Byrnes and Nickels. The faces of the disgruntled five hardly expressed the joy one would expect after such a brilliant victory.

"What is this," Gillen growled, "a one-man team?"

"Looks like it," Bob Emery muttered.

"Maybe we better turn in our uniforms," Burke said savagely.

"Putting on a real show, isn't he?" Nickels said bitterly.

"You'd think he won the game all by himself," Gillen said.

Byrnes was glowering evilly at Chip's back. "I'll fix his wagon," he promised. "Wait and see!"

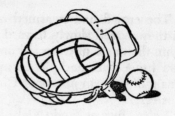

## CHAPTER 5

## ROCK'S WONDER BOY

MITZI SAVRILL had been watching the door for fifteen minutes. From the cashier's desk of George Grayson's State Drug, Mitzi had a clear view of the street and a perfect vantage point from which to observe the entire store, especially the soda fountain. This last, much to the delight of Soapy Smith. When Chip and Soapy rushed in, fresh out of the gym shower and fresh out of breath from hurrying to get to work on time, Mitzi glanced pointedly at the clock. Soapy got it right off and stopped to explain, but Chip hurried on to his storeroom post. Outwardly, Soapy was deeply apologetic. Secretly, he was delighted to have the opportunity of talking to the light of his life.

"It was a ten-inning game, Mitzi, and we won! We beat the varsity! I mean Chip did!"

"All *play* and no work—"

"We'll make up for it, Mitzi! Honest!"

The stern expression on the face of the little blue-eyed cashier softened. "I was only kidding," she said sweetly. "Congratulations!" Her violet-blue eyes followed Chip's hurrying figure. "Both of you," she added softly.

Soapy made the storeroom, somehow. Entering in a daze, he took off his jacket, hung it up, took it down again, put it on, and started for the door.

"Hey!" Chip called. "Where you going? The fountain, remember? You work here!"

"Oh, yes," Soapy replied. "She's wonderful!"

"So is State and getting an education and having a good job where you can watch the love of your life every night and having a boss like George Grayson who lets you play baseball and still draw a pay check every week. Pay check! Get it? Money! Pays rent and eats and buys neckties and—"

Soapy interrupted. "—And boxes of candy! Sweets for the sugar— Sure, I get it! See you later!"

Chip followed Soapy to the door and watched him proceed to the fountain. Soapy was the most popular soda jerk in town. Fred "Fireball" Finley shared the refreshment duties with Soapy and seemed oblivious to Soapy's approach until the addled catcher was just behind him. Then, Fireball deftly thrust out a leg and tripped his co-worker.

"What's that for?" Soapy demanded indignantly. "Didn't I win the game? Didn't I uphold the honor of the freshman class? Where would guys like you be if it wasn't for great ballplayers like me? Huh? Where?"

Fireball regarded Soapy gravely. "First, you tell me how guys like you could play baseball if it wasn't for guys like me."

Soapy's mood changed instantly. "I'm sorry, Fireball," he said, "I didn't really mean that. And I do appreciate the extra work you're doing so I can play. I'll make it up someway, honest!"

Fireball grinned. "Aw, I was kidding, Soapy. You know that! Skip it! You might try waiting on a few customers, though. I'm bushed. Seems like everybody on the campus wanted frosteds or sundaes or some of your freak specialties. Maybe it's spring!"

Soapy glanced across toward the cashier's desk and sighed. "I know," he said mournfully. "I know. Hey, how's your new heart throb?"

Finley punched Soapy in the ribs. "Swell girl, Soapy," he said earnestly. "Real swell! Her old man's a great guy, too."

"You're tellin' me! You oughta heard him rootin' at the game. I could hear him above everyone else. He's some fan!"

"Maybe too much of a fan."

Soapy bridled. "How can anyone be too much of a fan?" he demanded indignantly.

"Well, he's got a few responsibilities beside baseball, you know."

"Cynthia Ann?"

"Of course. It costs a lot of money to put a girl through college and running a big farm is no joke."

Finley's serious attitude sobered Soapy instantly. The big fellow was a dead ringer for Soapy, except that he was bigger and better looking. He had red hair, blue eyes, and packed two hundred and twenty pounds on his six-foot frame. Soapy winked an eye knowingly as he put an extra dipper of ice cream in the blonde's soda. "You're with it," he said. "Really with it! Right?"

Fireball nodded. "That's for sure!"

"Well, start holdin' your breath," Soapy warned. "Here she comes in all her glory—and with her old man!"

Jim Collins made straight for Soapy. "Congratulations, Smith! Great game! Where's Hilton? In the storeroom? Think it's all right to go on back? Just got to shake hands with that guy. I'll be right back, Cindy."

Cynthia Ann didn't even hear her father. She and Fireball were talking in low voices, heads close together, oblivious to everyone.

Chip was seated at the storeroom desk working on some perpetual inventory sheets when Collins knocked and opened the door. "Hiya, Chip! What a game! Boy, every fan in town is talking about you! Say, I'm throwing a steak dinner for the whole team at my house tomorrow right after practice. Can you make it?"

Chip shook his head. "Sorry, Mr. Collins. I have to work. Besides, I've got a lot of studying to do. Working and baseball and studies keep me hopping."

Collins was visibly disappointed. "Gee, Chip, I was counting on having the whole team there, especially you."

The big man lingered a little longer, trying to convince Chip that he ought to come for a little while. Cynthia Ann could drive Chip in from the farm right after enjoying a steak as thick as a dictionary. In the end, Collins regretfully gave up and made Chip promise he'd come out to the farm some Sunday for a special treat.

Soapy was busy behind the fountain. He was trying to serve everyone in sight so Fireball would have time to talk to his girl. But busy as he was, Soapy kept one of his big ears cocked in Fireball's direction. Soapy could tell Fireball was excited about something because he was speaking too fast and a little too loud.

"Why invite the whole team? Why does he have to do things like that? Especially when you have to do all the cooking."

"But I'm not doing all the cooking. Aunt Mary is going to help and a couple of the girls from Home Ec are coming out early tomorrow afternoon. Anyway, it isn't work, it's fun!"

"That's what I'm getting at—"

"Don't tell me you're jealous! Why don't you come, too?"

"I'm not jealous but I am worried about—well, about, the farm."

Cynthia Ann's face clouded and there was a short silence. Then Fireball said contritely, his voice filled with concern. "I'm sorry, Cynthia. I didn't mean to say that."

"That's all right, Fireball. I wish you'd come. We could have a lot of fun."

"But I'm not on the team and your father didn't invite me."

"I invited you. Besides, you're a better baseball player than anyone on the team. You didn't make the All-State baseball team just because you played quarterback on the football team!"

That remark brought Soapy about like a flash. "You mean you were an All-State ballplayer?" he demanded.

Finley was surprised but not at a loss for words where Soapy was concerned. "What big ears you have, junior," he said grimly.

Soapy wiggled his flaps appreciatively. "The better to hear you with, my darling," he said smugly. Then he remembered. "Hey, you never told me you played baseball!"

Finley raised an eyebrow in mock surprise. "Did I have to?"

"You tell me everything else."

Cynthia Ann was fingering the gold baseball which hung from the tiny chain strung around her neck. "He was All-State for two years," she said proudly, "and he turned down a big-league contract to come to college. From the Eagles!"

Finley was uncomfortable. "Didn't mean anything," he said, shrugging his shoulders.

The blonde broke up the conversation. "Since when did a black and white have *chocolate* ice cream in it?" she demanded.

Soapy was deeply apologetic. "These new scoops have been causing us all sorts of trouble," he explained. He reached into his pocket and produced a card. "Permit me to give you a rain check on your next guzzle fuzz," he said, bowing and placing the pasteboard on the counter.

"Why do you have the telephone number printed so large?" the blonde asked innocently.

"So your big beautiful eyes can read it easily," Soapy rejoined. "Especially big brown eyes, ahem!"

Finley began to hum in a low voice, "Five feet two, eyes of blue—"

Soapy cast a demoralized glance toward the cashier's desk and pivoted sharply away from the attractive customer. "Please," he hissed. "Shut up!"

Soapy ignored the blonde completely after Finley's warning, but his sharp eyes noted that she picked up the card. Fireball noticed that, too. After Collins and Cynthia Ann left, he began talking in a voice which carried clear across the store about employees who presented customers with their name cards.

"Please, Fireball," Soapy pleaded, "she'll hear you."

"That's what you get for eavesdropping," Fireball growled.

"I'll never do it again. Promise! Won't tell what you were talking about either!"

Soapy broke part of the promise that very night. But

he felt the end justified the means. Soapy was afraid that he had hurt Fireball's feelings and he was deeply concerned about the sacrifice the big fellow was making in taking the early shift week after week. Soapy decided to talk to Chip about Fireball.

Chip had the responsibility of closing the store and checking the inventory sheets each night and Soapy always waited for his friend. On the way home to Jefferson Dormitory, they talked baseball. Chip was surprised to learn that Finley had been an All-State ballplayer.

"I'll bet he's been eating his heart out all through spring practice," Chip said gravely. "How about that! All the time we were working out, he was coming in early and covering our work."

"*Our* work!" Soapy remonstrated. "You mean *my* work!"

"Same thing."

"Nuts! It doesn't have a thing to do with your job. You know something? Fireball's changed completely since the football trouble you and he had. Why, he never said a thing about being a good player when we were talkin' baseball. Some change from the guy who talked about nothing except Fireball Finley when we first met him."

"I wish I'd known," Chip said. "I wouldn't have let him talk me into going out for the team."

"His job has nothing to do with—"

"Oh, yes, it has! Remember there's two of us away from the job! We'll just have to make it up to him someway, that's all."

Soapy stopped short. "I know one way," he said excitedly. "It's not much but it will help. He'd like to go to Collins' for the steak dinner tomorrow night."

"That's easy," Chip said cheerfully. "I can work at

the fountain until he gets back. I'm way ahead on my work. We'll tell him tonight, O.K.?"

Jefferson is an extremely democratic dormitory. Maybe it is because most of the Jeffs are working all or part of their way through school. That may be the bond which makes Jeffs so loyal to one another and so proud of their dorm campus accomplishments. And it may be that Jeff has attracted a special kind of college student. The kind of youngsters who regard college as a steppingstone to real-life accomplishment; students who are looking far into the future, envisioning leadership in a particular field of the business of earning a living and providing for a family.

The rooms at Jeff are small. There isn't much space for anything except standard dormitory furniture, and each room is assigned to two frosh students. Yet, strange as it may seem, each cubicle has a definite personality of its own. Perhaps this is owing to the pin-ups which grace or distort the various walls (according to your personal likes or dislikes for such decorations) and perhaps it is owing to the bright curtains and colorful bedspreads the particular mother has selected to provide a touch of home for her son. Perhaps the occupants themselves have something to do with it and have lent a bit of their own personalities to give an atmosphere of lived-in warmth to the four walls.

Room 211 on the second floor is furnished simply enough but it is one of the most popular rooms in the building. The magnet is the strange combination of leadership and prankish fun. Chip Hilton, the president of Jeff, and Soapy Smith, the clown prince of the dorm, live in 211. Chip was elected unanimously last fall to the important post. Soapy just moved in and took charge of the fun life of everyone in the place. Soapy is that kind of guy.

Room 211 was ganged as soon as they turned on the light. It seemed to Chip that the whole dorm was trying to get into the room to congratulate him on the big victory. And all his protestations that he had done nothing fell on deaf ears. He was a Jeff man and he had won the game and he was the hero and that was that!

Chip liked it, of course. Who wouldn't? But it made him uncomfortable and he was glad when "lights out" sent his admirers trooping off to bed.

Biology lab kept him late the next afternoon and practice was well under way when he arrived. Rockwell was belting long flies to the outfield and the pitchers were limbering up in front of the grandstand.

Soapy was waiting with his big glove and Chip began to loosen up. Lefty Byrnes was throwing to Nickels nearby, and their sarcastic chuckles and low-voiced references to the Rock and the Wonder Boy brought Chip back to the problem yesterday's game had revealed. He was glad that Jim Collins had managed to get Henry Rockwell to agree to a short practice so the gang could get out to the farm on time.

Later, at the drugstore, he forgot the whole disagreeable matter when Fireball Finley flashed a grateful smile in the direction of Soapy and himself and took off for the Collins farm.

Mitzi Savrill had clipped the story of the dinner from the paper, and Soapy brought it over for Chip to read. Jim Collins was on the sports page again.

### JIM COLLINS PLAYS HOST TO FROSH BASEBALL SQUAD

Members of the colorful freshman baseball squad are to be honored with a steak dinner this evening at the Collins farm. Jim Collins, local baseball booster, has invited the players, managers, and Coach Henry Rockwell to the affair.

The Collins farm is one of the best in the county and has been the scene of many such parties in the past. Jim is known to every baseball player who has worn a State uniform during the past twenty years and the current freshman stars will get a terrific lift from the event.

Few of the present-day baseball stars know it, but Jim Collins was one of the greatest diamond performers ever to play baseball in this part of the state. In fact, State baseball and Jim Collins are usually mentioned in the same breath by local fans.

Members of the college male octet, directed by Billy Richmond, will be guests and will sing several num-bers. Other entertainment features will consist of Carmen and Carlos, featured dance team from the Silver Slipper; Fat Freddie Ferguson and his Campus Capers orchestra, and the showing of several baseball films.

Assisting in the preparation of the food will be Mrs. Martha Stanton, head dietician at the student union, and several members of the Home Economics Department of the college. Miss Cynthia Ann Collins will be in general charge of the affair.

A note of warning from this writer: "Take it easy on all that food, freshmen. You're playing the varsity tomorrow afternoon and they've sworn to eat nothing but spinach and carrots until they avenge yesterday's defeat! A word to the wise is . . ."

Soapy grunted. "Nuts!" he said. "We'll kill 'em!"

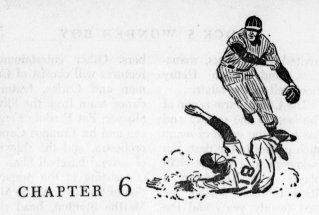

# CHAPTER 6

## THE BUNTING GAME

"Sure! Right over the fireplace!"

Soapy was intrigued. He listened quietly as Finley described the inscription which Jim Collins had placed over the mantel in the big farmhouse living room.

"'God bless our mortgaged home,'" Soapy repeated. "That's good! He must have a wonderful sense of humor."

"It isn't funny," Finley said shortly. "He's in debt up to his ears and Cynthia is worried sick about the mortgage payments. She wants to quit school and go to work."

"He wouldn't stand for that."

"What could he do?"

Soapy spread his hands in a helpless gesture. "Got me, pal. Go to work, I guess."

"And give up baseball? Uh, uh! Not him! All he thinks about is balls and strikes and hits and the old days. To listen to him, he was the best catcher that ever pulled on a monkey suit."

"Maybe he was!"

"Oh, sure!"

"How big you say the steaks were?"

"About the size of home plate!"

"Mmmmm. You have a good time?"

"And how! Thanks to you!"

"And Chip," Soapy added.

Finley sobered. "That reminds me—" he began. "Er, Chip ever have any trouble with Byrnes?"

Soapy hesitated and shook his head slowly. "Guess you couldn't call it trouble," he said. "Byrnes made a couple of mean remarks to Chip, but that's all."

"Well, anyway," Finley continued, "everything was swell until after the eats and Byrnes said he'd have to get the taxi back on the job. Mr. Collins said it was too bad guys like Chip and Byrnes had to work and then he said something about Chip being a clutch player. Byrnes sort of laughed then and said anyone could star if the coach saved him for the right spot. It looked like trouble for a minute. You know Cohen!"

Soapy nodded. He knew Biggie Cohen all right— knew that anyone who started anything with Chip Hilton was stepping on Biggie's big toes and that meant trouble with a big T. Soapy grinned. "Yeah, I know. What happened?"

"Well, nothing much. Biggie started toward Byrnes, but Nickels and Morris moved in between them, and Nickels whispered something to Byrnes and Lefty, then his gang all piled in the taxi and left. Mr. Collins was puzzled, but Cynthia fixed that by asking him to tell about the time he badgered a chucker he was catching into pitching a no-hitter."

Soapy was all ears. "A no-hitter? How? How'd he do it?"

"Well," Fireball continued, "seems like this chucker had a lot of stuff but no confidence. So Mr. Collins got the idea of kidding this guy into believing he was terrif. He kept telling him how fast he was and that the fast ball he was throwin' was so hard that Collins' glove hand swelled up so big he couldn't get it out of the catcher's mitt. So, in an important championship game, this pitcher was on the mound and Collins began giving him the business. The other team couldn't get a hit and the guy begins to get swell-headed and Collins starts to bear down on him, telling him he was a quitter and that the manager was going to pull him if he didn't start to pitch. This goes on for a few innings and the chucker is fit to be tied, wants to murder Collins. Still Collins keeps it up, according to his telling, and the guy is so mad at him that he pitches a no-hitter."

Fireball was enjoying Soapy's concentration. He grinned and continued. "That is, if you can believe my future father-in-law."

"What!" Soapy shouted, breaking the Number One library ruling and drawing a militant glare from the librarian with the severe hair-do and the bifocals. "Ya mean you're engaged?"

"*Shhhh*. Of course not! I'm just kidding. You want me to tell you the rest of the story or not?"

"Yeah, but—"

"No *buts!* Anyway, the upshot of the whole thing was that the pitcher didn't know Collins was using psychology until after the game, and they became fast friends. You like fish stories, Soapy?"

Soapy didn't answer. He was deep in thought. Fireball's story had given him an idea and Soapy toyed with it through History 21 and during the long afternoon while he was sitting in the bull pen.

Alumni Field was jammed and the Fence Busters took it in stride by getting off to a good start once again.

Hutch Kroll hit the first pitch of the ball game right back at the pitcher, the ball flying past Len Harris' legs, over second and on out into center field. Speed Morris laced a liner into right field and went on to second when varsity's right fielder, Lee Carter, made the long, futile throw to third in an attempt to nip Kroll. Bob Emery, a lefty hitter, caught one of Harris' portside hooks right on the nose and pulled it straight as a string to the right-field fence. Kroll and Morris scored, and Emery held up at second. Then, Biggie Cohen, playing the role of cleanup hitter according to the script, laced a two-two pitch clear over the right-field fence. The frosh were ahead 4 to 0 with no one down. Del Bennett called time and headed for the mound.

Jim Collins was in his favorite seat, surrounded as always, by the most rabid fans in the park. Collins had established himself as a real authority with this crowd. Especially after the Wednesday onslaught which the frosh had made on the varsity pitchers.

"Here we go again!" Collins yelled. "They're going to have to move the fences back for this gang!"

"It's only the first inning, Jim," someone reminded him.

"Pretty good start!" Collins retorted. "Guess those steaks I fed the kids last night hit the spot. Had everybody there but Hilton and Smith," he added proudly.

Chip was seated in the dugout. In the dressing room, just before the game, Rockwell had designated Chip as the starter for the final game. "If it's necessary, gang," Rockwell had said. "Personally, I think we'll sew it up this afternoon. Dean, you start. Nickels, catch—"

Lefty Byrnes and Flash Sparks were leaning on the railing of the frosh bull pen, watching the game. Silent Joe Maxim and Soapy were playing catch, leisurely throwing the ball back and forth, pausing from time to time to watch the developments in the game.

Soapy was strangely quiet. He scarcely opened his mouth, which was something very, very unusual for Soapy. Yes, Soapy was deep in thought, planning a psychological campaign.

"They're powdering the ball," Sparks exulted. "The gang's got Bennett worried. He's trying to save Rickard for tomorrow. Huh! He shoulda used him today. What's that they say about there bein' no tomorrow?"

"If our guys keep on like this, there won't be no tomorrow," Byrnes said lightly. "I'm sure pulling for that! Rockwell's got Hilton for the feature spot tomorrow again. And *that*, I would sure like to see spoiled!"

Sparks turned his head to study Byrnes. "You don't like Hilton, do you," he said.

"Like him! You crazy? How could anyone like that swell-headed grandstander?"

"I think you've got him wrong," Sparks protested. "I never met the guy until we started spring practice, but I watched him play football and basketball. He's got it! Seems like a pretty nice guy, too. One thing I know— he's one sweet ballplayer!"

"You're entitled to your own opinion," Byrnes said sullenly. "Anyone can star when the coach picks the spots."

"Well, there won't be any spots if he starts tomorrow. He'll be on his own all the way."

"On his own is right," Byrnes said cryptically.

The huddle on the mound disintegrated, leaving Harris to continue. Bennett had evidently decided to stay with the tall lefty. But there was activity in the varsity bull pen. Slim Burton and Ned Diston were throwing fast, warming up in a hurry. Hex Rickard, like

Chip, was watching the game from the dugout. Bennett had notified the press and everyone else that Rickard would be the starting pitcher for the third game. And Del had left no doubt in the minds of his listeners that he believed there would be a third game.

Belter Burke didn't get all the wood on the ball but he drove George Reed, out in center field, all the way back to the fence for the catch. Durley hit sharply to shortstop and was out by the proverbial whisker when Russ Merton made a perfect peg to first. Murph Gillen met one right on the nose, driving a lofty fly to left field, but Bill Bentley went back a mile to pull it in for the third out. Len Harris had survived, but the frosh had a big four-run lead.

The varsity led off with Russ Merton and the little shortstop worked Dean for a walk. Tubby Ryder singled, and Bill Bentley, power-hitting left fielder, pulled a shocker by laying a bunt to the left of the mound. Diz made the try at third, but he had been caught by surprise, and Merton beat the throw with ease. That loaded the bases and brought up George Reed, the varsity cleanup hitter. Reed swaggered up to the plate, big and powerful and confident. Pulling his bat through in a full practice swing, the rippling muscles of his bare forearms bulging with power, Reed seemed all set for a full swing.

Dean was cautious, got behind at two and no, and thoughtlessly laid one down the middle. Then, everyone except Del Bennett and Reed and the runners got a shock. Reed bunted! Merton was away with the pitch, and Dean, caught in the middle, waited too long to make a decision and ended up with the ball in his hand, never making a throw to any base.

Out in the frosh bull pen, Flash Sparks began to

burn them in to Soapy as he belatedly tried to get warmed up. Butch Harris, the upperclassmen's towering first sacker, powdered the first pitch and drove the ball straight as one of Sammy Snead's tee shots, up and out and over the four-forty-foot right-center fence. That cleared the bases and put the varsity out in front 5 to 4, and sent Diz Dean to the showers.

"Here we go," Byrnes said bitterly as Sparks started for the mound. "Setting the stage for Glamour Boy!"

Sparks wasn't ready and walked Carter. But he got a break when Minson drove a hard grounder between short and second. It looked as if the ball was in there for a hit, but Speed Morris came streaking across from deep short to scoop up the ball and relay it with an underhand toss to Kroll. Hutch made a perfect pivot and throw to Cohen for the double play. Widow Wilder popped up to Nickels and the frosh came trotting in, one run behind, but confident and cocky and eager for their licks and an opportunity to pulverize the ball.

Nick Nickels, looking big and as solid as a rock, sauntered up to the plate, smiling and confident. Nick looked at a ball and a strike, and then clocked the next pitch with the fat of the bat. The apple took off in a slow-rising flight which carried far over Bentley's head in left field, over the fence, and vanished somewhere in the forest of legs on the lacrosse field.

The fans cheered the burly catcher all around the circuit and Nickels came in smiling, doffing his cap as he crossed the plate. That evened it up at 5–5.

Sparks went down swinging. Kroll chopped a soft Texas leaguer over third base. Morris slashed a hard ground ball between first and second, but Tubby Ryder made a sensational stop, knocking the ball down and then throwing to Merton for the force at second. It was two away. Bob Emery, eager and trying too hard, wouldn't look them over and golfed a low inside hook to Bentley for an easy third out.

The game rolled on much after the Wednesday pattern. But there was a difference in the methods used to get the runs. The frosh were slugging away on their own whenever they were "ahead" of the pitcher. Rockwell was taking full advantage of the supreme confidence of his kids, playing the only cards at his disposal.

Del Bennett was using "hit" and "take" signs, the hit and run, the steal, the delayed steal (men on first and third), the double steal, the squeeze, and every trick in the book. And, for all it was worth, he was directing the bunting game at the frosh pitchers.

Both coaches were right. Rockwell's frosh just weren't capable of competing with the upperclassmen where "inside" baseball was concerned, but they were better hitters. Bennett had the better pitching, but his veterans couldn't compete with Rockwell's sluggers at the plate. It all added up to the kind of game the fans love; they got a kick out of the hitting of the kids and enjoyed a hundred opportunities to second-guess Bennett.

Sparks was getting a practical education with respect to fielding his position. Bennett's bunting game kept him busy. Too busy! Flash was having all kinds of trouble. So was Butcher Durley! Bennett was using the bunt as a hit-and-run play, sending the runner on first down on the second or third pitch. Biggie, Sparks, and Durley would come dashing in to play the ball and the hitter would lay it down the third-base line. The second baseman, Hutch Kroll, frequently got confused and tried to cover the steal. That left first open and Durley had no one to throw to. He usually froze where he had fielded the ball. Then the runner would go on to third. It was pretty to watch, hard to take.

Bennett was working another old trick. With first and second occupied, none away, a vet would fake a bunt to see how Butcher was going to react. If Durley showed that he was going to field the ball, Bennett would put on a double steal and the hitter would fake the bunt. When Durley dashed in to field the bunt and found there was no play, he would try to get back to the bag to cover and, more often than not, was in no position to take Nickels' throw. Morris tried to help Durley but that meant leaving his position too soon, and Bennett's place hitters promptly lined one through the hole. Occasionally a varsity hitter would push one past the charging Durley and then Morris was in trouble.

It was a busy afternoon for Rockwell's chuckers and infielders. In the eighth, with the bases loaded and no one down, Rockwell sent Sparks to the showers. No one would ever have known that Rockwell had debated his next move for a long time. It was not apparent in his decisive motion for Byrnes. Yet, the veteran coach was wondering if it was not giving the ill-tempered boy too much of a challenge. One thing was sure. A change had to be made if the game was to be won.

Rockwell had worked with boys all his life. He knew there came a time in the development of a youngster where the slack in the rope had to be tightened if the boy was to develop into a real ballplayer. He figured the time had now come with respect to Lefty Byrnes.

When Rockwell called, Byrnes put on an act. He was apparently surprised. He held up the game while he hurriedly threw a few extra pitches to Soapy before heading for the mound. And, on the way, he stopped to fix his shoestring, picked up a blade of grass, and kept tossing his glove restlessly from hand to hand as he slowly advanced. Every action evidenced his displeasure.

Most of the fans remembered Byrnes' former display of temper and were watching his approach with varying thoughts. Many had written off his display of poor sportsmanship on Wednesday as the usual idiosyncrasy attributed to a left-hander. Others were openly disgusted with the youngster. All were interested in observing his reaction to the present situation.

Jim Collins was typically optimistic. "Things will be a little different, now," Collins opined. "This big kid has the makings of one of the best in the game!"

"Didn't do a very good fielding job Wednesday," someone barked sarcastically.

"What's one error this early in the season!" Collins retorted.

"Doesn't mean a thing unless it gets to be a habit," a shrill voice observed.

"Since when is bein' temperamental a habit?"

"Temperament or temper?" the first fan demanded.

"I always thought a guy had to prove himself before he could afford to be temperamental," a third added.

"Some kids have to learn things the hard way," Collins said, sobering most of his personal badgerers. "It wouldn't hurt to remember he's just a kid."

It was too bad all the fans couldn't have heard Collins' last remark. They might have abstained from voicing their disapproval and restrained the chorus of boos which greeted Byrnes' approach to the rubber.

Rockwell greeted Byrnes nonchalantly. In fact, he was smiling and appeared completely relaxed. "Don't worry about it, kid. Just blaze that fast one of yours in there a little on the high side and see what happens."

Byrnes didn't look at Rockwell. He waited with his eyes fixed on the pitching plate on the toe of his left shoe until Rockwell turned away. Then he sniffed contemptuously and shrugged his shoulders.

"C'mon, Lefty," Nickels said understandingly. "Show him up! Make him like it!"

"Aw, what's the use! That guy won't give anyone but Hilton a break!"

"The heck with Hilton! The heck with Rockwell, too! How about the team! C'mon, let's win this one! Shoot! We're out in front by two runs! The weak end of the stick is up. Minson can't hit a curve, and Wilder's a sucker for anything inside. Burton doesn't even take the bat off his shoulder. C'mon, Lefty. This is your chance!"

In all justice to Byrnes, it should be said that he tried. But he hadn't brought himself up to the right emotional pitch. That was understandable, too. Byrnes had always been a starting pitcher, a star who had been able to meet his competition with absolute confidence. But he was up against a fine college ball club, a veteran team coached by an all-time big-league pro. Quite different from high school competition. The varsity was riding on a surge which had loaded the bases. There was no one down and they were determined to get those ducks off the pond.

Minson was long past due. He was bursting with desire to lace the old apple. But Bennett killed that ambition and called for the squeeze. Minnie responded beautifully and pushed one between Durley and Byrnes for his first hit of the game. Reed scored and all hands were safe. Byrnes had tried hard to reach the ball but couldn't make it. Morris came in fast and fielded the ball but his throw to first was late. The varsity was now one run behind with no one away.

Standing behind the rubber, Byrnes appeared calm. But he was seething inside. He turned to look contemptuously at Morris, and then faced Widow Wilder.

Widow was a picture of determination. He waited Lefty out, waited until he got the pitch he wanted. It was a two-two fast ball, letter high, and Wilder pulverized the pitch for his first real blow of the series. The ball cleared the right-field fence by twenty feet and the varsity was three runs ahead.

Byrnes got Burton on called strikes. Then he fanned Merton with a first-pitch called strike which split the plate, a fast ball around the wrists which Merton went for too late, and a sharp breaking hook which ducked under Russ's bat on the outside corner. Ryder hit the ball high in the air over the box, and Biggie waved Byrnes away and made the catch for the third out.

Rockwell, waiting in front of the bat rack, attempted to pat Byrnes on the back. But the dejected chucker swerved aside and ducked under the protecting roof of the dugout.

"We'll get 'em back, Lefty," Nickels said soothingly.

"Don't worry about it," Morris said. "We'll hit!"

"That's for sure," Cohen added. "We'll get you some runs!"

Del Bennett crossed them up. Bennett sent Ned Diston, his Number Two pitcher, in for the kill and the fast ball chucker set them down in order. The varsity didn't need the last turn at bat. They won the game 15 to 12, and evened the series at one game apiece.

Chip had suffered along with Byrnes during that hectic base-loaded inning and followed his teammates slowly up the hill to the field house. Most of the gang had been eager to get away from the field and had lit out for the showers with disgruntled hearts. At the gate leading to the field house, Chip passed Byrnes and

Nickels. He was ill at ease but couldn't resist an expression of sympathy.

"Tough luck, Lefty," he said. "We'll get 'em tomorrow."

Byrnes' face flushed with rage. "Natch," he said viciously. "Rockwell's Wonder Boy is pitching tomorrow!"

# CHAPTER 7

## PITCHERS' DUEL

Soapy Smith was a good student. The funster was an apt listener and possessed a wonderful capacity for absorbing information. He drank in every word in class and was able to retain the essential part of each lecture. Psychology I was his chief delight and Professor Engels was his favorite member of the faculty.

Soapy had co-operated in a number of Professor Engels' psychology tests, including participation as a hypnosis subject. Soapy liked the course, and, unknown to anyone, including Chip, his closest friend, was seriously considering the subject as a major in anticipation of a teaching career.

For the first time since the first semester exams, Soapy showed up behind State Drug's soda fountain with a textbook. Fireball was shocked and could scarcely believe his fountain mate was feeling right. He was deeply solicitous, but Soapy ignored him and snatched every opportunity to concentrate feverishly on the text.

Most of the customers attributed Soapy's subdued spirits to the loss of the game. But they were entirely wrong. Soapy was concentrating on a psychological angle which would have delighted Professor Engels. The unusual studious mood in which Soapy was steeped resulted in much inconvenience to sundry ice-cream connoisseurs who liked Soapy but were a bit fed up with the "new dipper" alibi.

Chip noticed Soapy's preoccupation when they were on their way home but let it pass. Chip had a few things on his own mind. First and foremost was tomorrow's championship game. Long after he and Soapy had turned in, Chip was thinking about the varsity hitters and their weaknesses. He tossed and turned all night, living through a nightmarish dream in which he couldn't get the varsity out in the very first inning of the game.

Soapy was first to awaken the following morning. He rushed to the window and anxiously surveyed the perfect sky. That was important news and Soapy began broadcasting. "Hey, Chipper! Wake up! Sunshine! Gobs of it! Pitcher's delight! Hey, that's a good name for a sundae! Have to remember that! C'mon, hit the deck! There's gonna be a million fans out there this afternoon."

Soapy's estimate was slightly exaggerated, but there was a capacity crowd on hand at two o'clock when the varsity trotted out on the field to carry on where they had left off the previous afternoon. Not that Soapy was any longer interested in spectators. No, Soapy had only one objective and that was concerned with Chip Hilton. During the warm-up in front of the grandstand, Soapy kept chattering away, setting his pal up for the big test. Chip hadn't been paying too much attention to Soapy, but the redhead's persistency eventually got his attention.

"I never saw you faster, Chip," Soapy said, shaking

his head. "Boy, lookit my hand! You're really burnin' 'em in today! And that was only warmin' up. Wish I had a piece of beefsteak—"

Chip grinned disarmingly. "You hungry?"

"Aw, Chip," Soapy protested. "You know what I mean. To put in my glove."

"I know, Soapy. Anyway, you're right. I never felt better."

Soapy looked at Chip suspiciously. Chip never bragged and the statement chilled Soapy. But only for a second.

"Hope none of those guys get in the way of one of your hard ones," Soapy continued worriedly. "Boy, they better be wearin' helmets! Think I ought to tell Bennett?"

"Oh, I don't think so. He probably knows what he's doing."

The umpire's "play ball" sent them into the dugout then and temporarily checked the discussion. But not for long. Soapy went right back to work as soon as they were seated.

Hex Rickard looked extremely fast to Chip. The tall lefty's hard ball seemed to have a hop on it and Widow Wilder was making sure each pitch cracked like a fast ball meeting the fat of Mickey Mantle's bat.

In fact, Chip thought the whole varsity looked unusually sharp. The ball went flying around the horn and across the diamond and back again without a slip. The fast, hard pegs and the accuracy of the throws drew a big round of applause from the fans.

Hutch Kroll led off, batting from the right-hand side of the plate. Hutch tried to work Rickard for a walk. It was a vain effort. Hex wasted nothing. He kept bearing down from the first pitch. He dropped them down around the stocky second baseman's knees and forced him to bounce a one-and-two pitch back to the mound. It was an easy out and a bad start. Kroll was tough up there, an ideal lead-off man, and so far in the series, he had set the pace.

Morris had always been weak against any sort of a curve and it was evident that the Widow and Hex were aware of the fact. Rickard's formula was simple. He drove Speed back from the plate and fed him a sharp hook. Then he drove him back again with an inside pitch and came back with a twisting curve which looked like a cunny-thumb roundhouse. Speed snapped at the bait but never touched the ball.

Bob Emery liked the fast ones, liked them high or low. The tall, wiry center fielder stood in the extreme rear of the batter's box and made a pitcher work. Rickard worked Bob with the teasers, the hook, the sweeping curve, the under-the-hands screw ball, and a flippety-flop knuckler which seemed to come out of nowhere across the plate. Emery, off balance, slugged away, but the best he could do was a short, lazy fly to right which Lee Carter gobbled in for the third out.

The fans gave Rickard a good hand, but when Chip walked out to the mound, they nearly tore down the stands. Cheering, stomping their feet, and applauding, they told Chip exactly how they felt about his play during the series. They hadn't forgotten that first game!

Jim Collins, on his feet and yelling his head off, nearly kicked a hole in the back of the seat directly ahead. The occupant was forced to stand up in self-protection. He turned around, exasperation written all over his face.

"You crazy?" the angry man shouted, trying to make himself heard above the crowd roar.

Collins nodded happily. "And how!" he shouted back. "He sure is a daisy! Best chucker in the country! Powders the apple, too!" He turned back to look at the diamond. "Yea-*aaaaaa!*"

Gee-Gee Gray, up in the announcer's booth, was yaking away, the words spilling from his mouth like the keys of a flying typewriter. Gee-Gee was in his element, broadcasting the game he loved.

"—And here comes the kid now! Coming out for the warm-up throws. It's a tough spot for a kid. Listen to the crowd! The fans like this youngster! This reporter likes him too.

"This is a crucial game. By the way, some of you fans may be wondering why the varsity has been the home team and has had the last licks in the series. Well, seems like it's one of State's sports traditions—the team which wins the series the preceding year becomes the home team the following year. The freshman haven't won the series for sixteen years. Most of us attribute that to the arrival of Del Bennett on the State campus as the head baseball coach.

"Right now, your old Gee-Gee would like to go out on a limb. Yep—I want to predict that next year's frosh will bat last in the pre-season series. Why? That's easy! Because the greatest kid chucker ol' Gee-Gee ever saw has finished his five warm-up pitches and is set to go to work. Yep—ol' Gee-Gee is backing the kid. The frosh catcher, Smith, has pegged the ball down to second base—and I mean pegged. This Smith can really throw that old apple to the bases. Hilton's got the ball now and here comes the best lead-off guy in college baseball today—Russ Merton—"

Lefty Byrnes and Flash Sparks had been loosening up, throwing the ball to Nickels in the frosh bull pen.

When the frosh took the field and Chip headed for the mound, the burst of applause carried clear to the end of the field, echoing again and again. Byrnes turned to watch and was joined by Sparks and Nickels.

Flash glanced at Byrnes when the cheers died down, noting the grim expression which clouded the lefty's face. And there was a mischievous gleam in Sparks' eyes when he spoke. "You see the *Herald* this morning?"

Byrnes shook his head and Sparks continued, "Bill Bell said Hilton was the best all-around frosh athlete in the history of the school."

Byrnes grunted disdainfully. "Bill Bell! What's that old goat know about sports?"

"He's the sports editor!"

"So what! Anyone with a drag with the owner of a paper can be the sports editor."

"Don't know about that! Anyway, Bell's been with the *Herald* for thirty years."

"What's that got to do with it?"

"Why, even a moron would learn something about sports after writing 'em for thirty years. Bell said he wouldn't be surprised if Hilton whitewashed the varsity. Said most all pitchers were ahead of the hitters this early in the season and that Hilton wasn't just any pitcher."

Byrnes glanced meaningly at Nickels. "He might have a surprise coming before the season's over."

"Yeah," Nickels added. "Lots of flowers bloom just in the spring."

Sparks glanced at the roommates curiously but said nothing. That didn't mean he wasn't thinking. Flash Sparks was a happy-go-lucky sort of fellow, an outstanding chucker in his own right. But Flash believed in giving credit where credit was due and he agreed with Bill

Bell. Flash recognized Chip's ability and bore him no ill feelings, even though they were rivals for a starting berth. Sparks couldn't understand why Byrnes and Nickels were so antagonistic. After an awkward silence, he shrugged his shoulders and concentrated on the action.

Russ Merton was a cocky little guy. He stood less than five-seven, and when he crouched at the plate, the strike zone all but vanished. But that wasn't all. Merton crowded forward and kept his head bobbing and weaving over the plate.

Chip was worried about Merton's head and threw everything overhand, keeping them low. He fed Russ a fast ball, a screw ball, and a hook. The two youngsters dueled away until it was the full count. Then Chip came in with a low, fast ball and Russ hit the ball hard. But it was on the ground, a high hopper which Butcher Durley took chest-high and clotheslined across to Cohen. Merton was out by thirty feet.

Tubby Ryder looked like Durley. If anything, he was shorter and stockier than Butcher. The husky hot-corner guardian stood about five-six and had an eagle eye. One had to put the ball right through the middle to tempt Tubby. Chip put it through the middle for the "take" pitch and then tried a low outside hook which Tubby watched impassively, ignoring it completely. Chip figured Ryder would go for the one and one and blazed it down with all the speed at his command. Tubby swung hard but topped the hard-breaking ball toward second. Hutch Kroll took the streaker and tossed the ball to Cohen for out number two.

That brought up Bill Bentley, and Soapy called time. Advancing to the mound, Soapy practically rubbed noses with Chip while he talked. Ostensibly, Bentley was the subject of the discussion. Actually, Soapy was complaining about his hand.

"Gee, Chip, I've got to do something about this glove. I never knew you to throw so hard. Merton and Ryder hit the ball because they couldn't get the bat out of the way. You be careful where you're throwin', cause if you hit anyone today, you'll break an arm or something. I'm gonna ask for a new ball. This one's got a blem—a blem—a spot on it and I can hardly see it."

Chip smiled understandingly. "I know, Soapy, I know. I never threw so hard in my life. My arm feels like a rubber band. I wonder what's come over me. I never felt like this before."

Soapy was grinning widely as he hustled back to the plate. He was mentally patting himself on the back. "It's workin'," he muttered gleefully. "It's workin'!"

"What's that?" the umpire demanded, glaring suspiciously at Soapy. "You talking to me?"

"Er, what's that?" Soapy echoed. "Oh, no, sir! I was just talkin' to myself, sir. Sir, can we have a new ball, sir? I can't see the one we're usin'."

"Now look here," the umpire thundered. "You just cut out that funny stuff and play ball. Understand?"

Soapy nodded. "Yes, sir," he said. But he didn't mean it. He wasn't cutting out anything! Not while Chip was co-operating so beautifully! He only hoped Professor Engels was in the stands.

Bentley, batting lefty, didn't have any trouble seeing the ball. He hit the first pitch! It was an inside hook which the left fielder caught high on the handle and looped over third. It looked as if the ball might drop in for a hit, but Morris showed the fans how he got his nickname by darting swiftly to his right and making an almost impossible running backhand catch. Speed stabbed at the looper just before it hit the ground and tumbled head over heels. But he held the ball! Chip breathed a sigh and trotted across the base line to pat the speedster on the back and walk with him to the dugout. Speed got a big hand.

It was that kind of ball game all the way. The frosh hit the ball every inning, but Rickard's stuff was breaking, and solid blows were few and far between. The frosh knicked him for three singles but none produced a run. Chip had hurled perfect ball. He hadn't allowed a hit. Soapy was bursting with importance and joy. He could scarcely restrain the urge to tell someone, just anyone, his secret.

The yearlings got men on base time after time but they couldn't score. With a duck on the pond, they'd hit a terrific grounder which a varsity infielder would somehow manage to field. With no one on, someone would hit a hard ball to the outfield, but it would head straight for one of the varsity outfielders as if it had eyes.

Biggie Cohen hit one over the right-field fence in the sixth, inches to the right of the foul-line marker. In the seventh, Chip, batting righty against Rickard's darting speed ball, hit one a mile into left field. But Bill Bentley called on all of his tremendous speed to make a sensational over-the-shoulder catch.

Del Bennett tried his bunt game, but Chip chilled that strategy, covering the area in front of the plate like a blanket and throwing out every hitter who laid one down.

So the game rocked along, through the ninth and into the top of the tenth. Rickard struck Durley out with three fast ones. Then, for the first time, his control slipped and he walked Gillen. Rockwell gambled then, called for time, and sent for Nickels to pinch-hit for Soapy.

"Surprise, surprise," Byrnes sneered, when Nickels started for the diamond. "About time the guy quit playing favorites. Must really want to win the game."

Rockwell wanted to win the game, all right. And he wasn't playing favorites or safe or anything but heads-up baseball. He had made up his mind to sacrifice Gillen to second and leave it up to Chip to win his own game. He stopped Nickels at the third-base coaching box and gave him his instructions, talking softly so he wouldn't be heard.

"Wait for a good one and lay it down. Rickard probably will figure you for the sacrifice or Gillen for the steal. He won't give you anything good, that's for sure. Look them over, and then, when he has to come in with a fat one—lay it down! O.K., boy, it's up to you. Push Gillen along and Chip will bring him in. He'll hit!"

Nickels turned away without a word and headed for the bat rack. "Hilton again," he growled. "Always Hilton! *He* can hit— Huh!"

## CHAPTER 8

## KNUCKLE-BALL PITCH

NICK NICKELS had a good eye. He was a consistent .300 hitter and hit the long ball. He worked Rickard for a two-and-no count and then stepped out of the box and eyed Rockwell in the coaching box at third base. Rockwell turned his back, indicating no change in the sign, and Nickels stepped back up to the plate.

Rickard delivered and Nickels shocked Rockwell and every frosh player in the dugout when he swung viciously at the pitch. It was a letter-high control pitch and Nickels cut under the ball, sending a high foul back to the screen. Widow Wilder flipped off his mask and scurried back to take the pop-up for out number two. Gillen was still anchored at first.

Rockwell rushed in from the coaching box and met Nickels in front of the dugout. Rock was almost speechless. "What happened?" the flustered coach demanded. "How come?"

Nickels didn't answer but began strapping on his shin guards.

Rockwell was puzzled. "What were you thinking

about? You deliberately crossed up the play! Why?"

Nickels finished buckling the shin guards and straightened up. But he didn't meet Rockwell's eyes. He pulled the chest protector over his head and stood there without saying a word.

Rockwell drew a deep breath and glanced beyond Nickels to Chip who was waiting in the on-deck circle. "All right," he said resignedly, gesturing Chip toward the plate, "you're on your own. Two away, remember."

Nickels ducked into the dugout, and Rockwell, still bewildered, hustled back to the coaching box.

Chip had a healthy respect for Rickard. The lanky southpaw worked the corners, avoided a fat pitch, and studied every hitter. Rickard had a healthy respect for Chip Hilton's hitting ability especially. Hex hadn't forgotten Chip's game-winning home run off Diston and, more recently, he remembered the fast ball Chip had tagged in the seventh. Now, Hex looked steadily at the varsity dugout, waiting for Del Bennett to decide whether he should issue Chip an intentional pass or work on him. Bennett spread his hands, palms up. That left it up to Rickard and he decided to pitch. "The kid *has* to be tired," Hex told himself. "I'll strike him out!"

Chip took the first pitch for a called strike. He watched a hook go by when it broke inches inside for a ball. And he got behind when he fouled another inside curve off the handle. Rickard decided to get it over and came in with an overhand fast ball between the belt and the knees. Chip belted it, golfed it in a high, whirling bender which headed out toward right center and curved clear to the right-field fence, banging against the boards inches inside the foul line.

Every fan in the park was on his feet, shifting his eyes between Lee Carter chasing the ball in the right corner of the field to Murph Gillen racing around the bases. Rockwell was a whirling turnstile in the coaching box, waving Gillen home.

The throw and Gillen and Wilder all converged at the plate, but Murph slid under and across before Widow Wilder tagged him, and the frosh had their first run. Chip pulled up at third.

Hutch Kroll hit the first pitch hard, but it was a straightaway fly ball which George Reed gobbled in for the third out. It didn't seem too important with that big one standing out as prominently as a black eye among all the zeros on the scoreboard.

Soapy checked Nickels when his rival started for the plate. "Chip's as smooth as a glove, Nick," he said cordially. "He'll put it right where you want it."

"Oh, sure!" Nickels said shortly.

The surly receiver made no attempt to check the signs with Chip. He simply squatted behind the plate and gave the sign for a fast ball. Chip shook it off. He had Lee Carter figured to a T. Carter batted from the right side of the plate and liked the hard one. Nickels then called for a hook and Chip slipped a called strike across on the inside.

Then Chip got a big surprise. Nickels burned the ball back to the mound on Chip's right side. The vicious throw was unexpected and Chip went for the ball without thinking, partly catching it with his throwing hand. The impact on his bare hand resulted in a sharp numbing sensation which was almost unbearable. But Chip controlled his impulse to give in to the pain and walked slowly behind the mound.

"That won't happen again, mister," Chip breathed. Standing there with his hands behind his back, he clenched and unclenched his fist in an attempt to get some feeling into his fingers. But when he tried to grip the ball his fingers would not respond. "Time," he called. "Time!"

Henry Rockwell had keen, black eyes. And he used them. Rock didn't miss much on a baseball field. He had seen the unnecessarily hard return which Nickels made and the fleeting expression of pain on Chip's face when he caught the ball. And he had been relieved when Chip gave no indication of injury. Now he was alarmed. Chip wouldn't call time unless he was badly hurt. Rockwell was out on the field almost as soon as the umpire raised his hands to stop play. Soapy was right behind him.

Chip clamped his glove under his left arm and looked at his throwing hand for the first time. "No wonder," he muttered. "No wonder."

The middle finger was bent almost all the way back. It was incongruously out of place. And the pain was intense. Before he could do anything about it, he was surrounded.

"Oh, oh," Biggie said. "Here's trouble."

"Not much," Chip said. "Here, pull it back in place."

Biggie recoiled. "Not me!"

"Nor anyone else!" Rockwell interrupted. "We'll let a doctor take care of that!"

"It's all right, Coach," Chip remonstrated. "It's only out of place."

The varsity dugout had stilled and the fans had quieted, except for a chorus of questions, answers, and sundry opinions. Del Bennett was out on the field now, accompanied by the varsity physician, Dr. Mike Terring. Terring took charge.

"Hold still, Chip," he said. "This will only take a second."

There was a little snap and Chip felt a quick spasm of pain and then relief. "That's fine," he said. "I'll be all right now."

Henry Rockwell was watching anxiously. "How about it, Doc?" he asked apprehensively. "Can he go on?"

Terring made no reply. He was exploring the injury with practiced hands, gently pressing the finger with his thumb, probing for a fracture.

Rockwell was undecided. Under ordinary circumstances he would have unhesitatingly sent Chip to the dugout. But this was different. Rock had several reasons for his desire to let Chip finish this game.

Soapy was concentrating. His lips moved soundlessly as he called on his newly found power for help. Soapy had his own particular reason for wanting Chip to carry on.

"Try to bend the finger, Chip," Terring suggested.

Chip tried, but it was no go. The finger had puffed up, now, and was as stiff as a board. "I can't move it much, Doc," Chip said quietly. "But I don't think it will mean much when I throw."

Terring smiled. "Gonna use knucklers exclusively?"

Chip nodded. "I might!"

"All right, Hank," Terring said. "I'll tape it up and you can leave him in the game if you wish. It won't hurt the finger if he can throw."

"I can throw!" Chip said grimly.

"By the way," Terring said, "you report to me in the training room right after you shower. I want to take an X ray." He turned to Rockwell. "It's just a stove, Hank, but I want to be sure. You can use him. That splint will protect the finger."

"O.K., Chipper," Rockwell agreed. "Give it a try."

Nickels was standing on the fringe of the group and

Biggie Cohen edged around until he was close beside the burly receiver. "Listen, Nickels," Biggie said gently, "you watch how you throw that ball back to the pitcher. Understand? You understand what I'm talking about?"

Nickels nodded and turned away, but his troubles weren't over. Rockwell took him by the arm and walked him back to the plate. Keeping a firm grip on the big fellow's arm, Rockwell spoke rapidly and sternly. "That was a dirty trick, Nickels. Stay in the game, but it's your last chance. Don't ever cross me up again on the signs, and you make sure you throw that ball back to the pitcher the way it ought to be thrown back. On the *glove-hand* side."

The fans knew what had happened, and they gave Chip a tremendous round of applause when it was apparent that he was going to continue. The varsity players joined in that hand, too.

With the count on Carter at no balls and one strike, Nickels squatted and gave the sign for a fast ball. Chip shook that off, not too sure he could throw the ball at all, much less a fast ball. They settled on a curve and Chip breathed a little prayer as he delivered the ball. Miraculously it headed for the plate, but there was nothing on the pitch, and Carter stepped into it as though it was a batting-practice throw.

There was a sharp crack and the ball took off like a flash of light down the left-field foul line. It was a fair ball and Belter Burke got on his horse and tore toward the fence without looking back. Belter never broke stride, never turned his head until the precise instant the ball arrived. Then he threw up his glove hand and made the catch over his shoulder, running at full speed. The fans gave the big outfielder a terrific hand.

Chip had been massaging his finger while the ball

was in the air and he was glad that Speed took the throw from Burke and trotted in with the ball.

"Bear down, Chipper," Speed pleaded. "Only two to go!"

Minnie Minson had big hands, strong arms, and powerful shoulders. And he liked a long bat. Chip remembered precisely what he had thrown to the husky third baseman Wednesday but he was afraid to try the screw ball, afraid it might get away. But the curve hadn't even been a good excuse. Then he remembered Doc Terring's remark. Well, he'd try it! He'd feed them knucklers.

Minson was waiting for the speed ball and let the first one go by for a called strike. Then Chip got another surprise. Nickels walked out in front of the plate and almost startled Chip by chortling, "Atta baby, big boy! Throw it in here!" Then Nick tossed the ball back on the glove side and walked slowly back to his position. And he took a long time getting set. It was evident to everyone that Nickels was using up all the time he could.

Chip welcomed the delay, his fingers were feeling better all the time. He kept shaking off the signs until Nickels got around to the knuckle ball again. Minson swung at the wobbly ball with all his might and missed. But the effort brought a mighty "Ah" from the stands.

Nickels was wise, now. He started the signs with the knuckler and Chip nodded. Minson was dug in, hoping for the fast ball. Chip faked it for all he was worth. The ball left his hand and shot up and out and down just as it had on Wednesday. And just as before, Minson checked his swing and then tried to murder the ball. He missed it by a mile. That made it two away and the frosh were one out away from a great victory.

Jim Collins was praising Chip to the skies. "Imagine that kid," he was yelling at everyone within hearing distance. "Imagine him pitching with a busted hand. You guys see the stuff on that knuckler? You see how he can control it? Bet there haven't been five pitchers in the history of the game who could control a knuckler."

Nickels burned the ball down to first after the strikeout, and while it went winging around the infield, Chip was refreshing his memory on Wilder. Widow Wilder was a switch hitter but he liked to bat righty. Maybe he could coax the knuckler low on the outside if Wilder hit from the third-base side of the plate.

Wilder took quite a while choosing a bat and then walked up to the righty side of the plate. Chip faked the fast ball but it was a wasted effort. Bennett had figured it out and knew now that Chip couldn't throw anything but the knuckler and Wilder was looking for it. Chip let it go, anyway, and Widow timed his swing perfectly. But he missed the ball. The knuckler is an unpredictable pitch as the ball follows no prescribed course. One time it bobs left, the next to the right.

Wilder stepped angrily out of the box. Then, on a sudden hunch, he made a great show of moving around to the first-base side of the plate. Chip didn't mind. He came in again with the knuckler and this time Wilder hit it—hit what most fans call a "loud foul." The ball floated up in the air along the first-base foul line and into the bleachers.

Nickels took the new ball from the umpire and sent it around the horn by way of Cohen, then back to Cohen and over to Chip. Once more Chip put all of his hopes and his back and his arm and his wrist into the knuckle ball. The ball flashed up and out and then darted down and bounced on the ground and across the plate and careened off Nickels' shin guards. Wilder swung so hard he nearly fell, but he missed the ball a mile. Widow was so nonplused that he forgot to run. And while he was standing there berating himself, oblivious to his teammates' pleadings to "run," Nickels retrieved the ball and tagged him out.

The frosh had won the series. Chip Hilton had a thirteen strike-out victory—and a *no-hitter!*

## CHAPTER 9

## SWITCH CHUCKER

STATE DRUG was jammed. Every baseball fan in town and every freshman in school wanted to see Chip Hilton. Chip had busied himself in the storeroom, thankful that he could keep out of sight. But Mitzi Savrill always had an eye out for business and drew George Grayson's attention to the "three-deep" crowd standing in front of the fountain. In her subtle manner, she made mention of the fact that Chip had pitched a no-hitter. That did it! Grayson chalked up another triumph for his petite genius and in a few minutes Chip was behind the fountain.

Chip's appearance created such a disturbance that pedestrians couldn't restrain their curiosity and crowded inside to add to the confusion. Soapy was doing a landslide business with State Drug's newest concoction, "Pitcher's Delight," but he took time out to lead a "Yea—Hilton! Yea—Chip! Yea—Chip Hilton!"

At closing time Chip got another tribute. A tribute engineered by Mitzi Savrill and backed by George Grayson. While Chip was filling-in at the fountain, Mrs.

Grayson was supervising preparations in the store-room for an informal staff party in the no-hitter hero's honor.

Chip was overwhelmed. He'd been ganged by most of the frosh in the dressing room after the game and tossed into the shower. Then tonight he'd been on the receiving end of congratulations at the fountain. Now he had to go all through it again. "Gosh," he protested, "I didn't do anything! Why, if Burke and Speed and Soapy and Biggie and all the gang hadn't played such a bang-up defensive game I'd probably been knocked out of the box."

Nobody got the idea that Chip was displeased. Far from it. But he honestly felt that his teammates weren't getting enough credit for the victory. He was glad when it was over and he was on his way home with Soapy.

Soapy was bubbling over. He just had to tell Chip the big secret. "Chipper," he said haltingly, "you know Prof Engels and his theories about autosuggestion and thought transmission and all that stuff—"

Chip grinned delightedly. "Yes, I know, Soapy."

"Well, I tried it today. I hope you don't mind. I was puttin' all that stuff in operation from the very beginning. Guess I sorta fibbed to you about my hand and everything, but I was determined you'd get a no-hitter. And, well, I guess the means justify the end—or whatever it is—and I hope you'll forget it."

"Sure, Soapy," Chip said soberly. "Think nothing of it."

Dormitory rules were a fetish with Pete Randolph, Jeff's building super. Pete never deviated from the rules. Lights were supposed to be out at midnight and out they went. Period!

That was the reason Jeff's president got such a shock

just as he and Soapy entered the hall. Every light on the first floor suddenly flashed on and a hundred voices crashed out with a cheer.

"Yea—Hilton! Yea—Jeff! Yea—Jeff's Hilton!"

Chip never did learn how they managed it, but Jeff threw a big midnight dorm party and Pete Randolph was right in the middle of it. Hot dogs, cokes, pie, cake, and every edible imaginable graced the buffet table. The celebration lasted a full hour.

Chip was exhausted when he finally escaped, but as he trudged up the stairs to the second floor, he could hear Soapy explaining the part psychology had played in victories such as today's shutout no-hitter.

Chip chuckled as he undressed in the dark. Soapy was a great guy and he wouldn't hurt him for the world. Fireball Finley had told him the Collins psychology story before he spilled it to Soapy. Chip grinned again. He'd have to be sure to check with Fireball—have to be sure Soapy didn't find out that he knew the Collins psychology story by heart.

Soapy was right on the ball Sunday morning. The redhead was waiting for the newsboy and grabbed one of Jeff's sixty-odd papers and dashed up the stairs two at a time. It didn't take him long to find the object of his search. It was stretched across the top of the first page of the sports section.

"Chip! Wake up! Lookit this!"

### HILTON WINS OWN GAME AND CAMPUS CHAMPIONSHIP
#### Pitches No-Hitter, Wins 1–0

##### By BILL BELL

William "Chip" Hilton, freshman star hurler, won his own game yesterday afternoon at Alumni Field

1–0. With two down in the top of the tenth and Murph Gillen on first base, Hilton connected for a three-bagger which drove in the lone tally of the game.

It was a brilliant personal victory for the young hurler who pitched through the last frame with an injured hand. Hilton struck out the last two batters to face him to register thirteen strike-outs in ten innings.

Hex Rickard pitched a steady game for the varsity and received fine support from his teammates, but he couldn't match the peerless pitching of Coach Rockwell's freshman phenom.

Hilton gets credit for both of the frosh victories, and as a result of his performance in the campus championship series, ranks as the Number One pitcher on the campus. Young Hilton not only did a first-rate whitewash job of the varsity hitters, but he himself hit brilliantly in the clutch, winning both games with timely blows.

"That's terrible," Chip groaned. "What will the rest of the fellows think? Holy smokes, that reads as though I won the game all by myself."

"You did," Soapy said firmly. "Wait, there's more—"

"Please, Soapy. I don't want to hear it. Doesn't Bell say anything about the other guys?"

"Not much! Why should he?"

"Now you're being silly."

The longer the argument continued, the less ground Chip gained. He finally gave up, taking recourse in his books and study.

There were several other readers who wouldn't have sided with Chip Hilton in anything except his side of the argument with Soapy. Lefty Byrnes was angrily berating Bill Bell and Chip Hilton and Henry Rockwell. And his listeners agreed with everything he said. Nick Nickels, Belter Burke, and Murph Gillen were sore, good and sore.

"We might as well hand in our uniforms," Burke said bitterly.

"That's right," Murph Gillen agreed. "Why don't we?"

"I wouldn't give Rockwell and Glamour Boy that much satisfaction," Byrnes said stubbornly. "There are other ways—"

"What other ways?" Nickels asked.

"Just ways," Byrnes said evasively. "Stick around and you'll find out."

An athlete who enjoys sports fame is a magnet for all sorts of fans. Chip was in the limelight because of his baseball prowess and there wasn't anything he could do about it. The telephone rang all morning with calls from close, and not so close, friends and acquaintances who wanted to congratulate him. Right after lunch, Jim Collins showed up in his car with Fireball Finley and practically abducted Chip and Soapy.

"You promised," Collins said. "Remember? Remember you said you'd come out to the farm the first Sunday you had a chance. Well, this is the first Sunday. Bring your books."

Later, Chip was glad Jim Collins had called for him. The old homestead and the barns were slightly run-down, but the meadows, pastures, and woodlands were leafing out with the beautiful greens spring endows so lavishly and it was gorgeous. The peaceful quiet of the country was a welcome change from Chip's busy college life, and the homey friendliness of Jim Collins and Cynthia Ann was heart-warming. Chip was genuinely sorry when it was time to go home.

Chip got the hero treatment all day Monday from his fellow students. After a while he gave up trying to be modest. He accepted the praise for what it was worth and tried to give as much credit as possible to his teammates. He was glad when he had finished with his last class and could head for Doc Terring's office.

Terring was all smiles. "It's O.K., Chip. No break. But you'll have to go easy on the throwing for a few days. I told Rockwell.

"Now, let me take that splint off and tape it up. Don't want to see you lose your batting eye. By the way, when you're hitting, grip the bat. Don't baby that finger. The more you use it, except for throwing, the quicker it will heal. All right?"

Chip could feel the tension as soon as he entered the dressing room. Nothing was said, but there was a feeling present which was as expressive as words would have been. The usual clubhouse banter was missing, there were no wisecracks, not much talking of any kind. Biggie and Soapy tried to break through the barrier by praising Belter Burke's great catch and Gillen's base running, but the response was without warmth.

Henry Rockwell sensed the trouble as soon as the players reported on the practice field. Rock knew the signs. He had met this problem innumerable times during his thirty years of coaching. His antidote was simple: "Bear down and keep them busy. Make them hustle for their jobs."

The wily coach went right to work, wasting no time on compliments. "Let's go! Infielders over here in two rows for a little pepper ball, outfielders to the sliding pit. Pitchers and catchers loosen up over there in front of the bleachers. Hilton, you fall in with the outfielders."

Chip liked the way the coach handled the situation. He took his turn in the sliding pit, protecting his finger, but putting everything he had into the slides.

Rockwell was thorough. He made a fellow come in on

the left and the right with the hook; made him take off
with both feet driving for the bag to counter a blocked
base, and work on getting back to a base with a fall-
away.

It was a tough workout. Ballplayers always gripe
about the "tough" coach, the coach who bears down,
who makes them work hard. But that's the coach they
respect and remember longest. Rockwell was remembered a long time by any player who worked under
the taskmaster.

After half an hour, Rockwell ordered the infielders to
the sliding pit and sent the outfielders to the diamond
for some base running and sign practice.

A scattering of spectators and fans began to show up
about this time in the bleachers, and Jim Collins was
among those present. As usual, Collins called out a loud
hello to every player in sight. Jim called them by their
first names and fairly exuded pride in the fact that he
was a personal friend of each of the youngsters. The big
farmer had a way with kids. A lot of youngsters could
have testified to that trait. Jim was a real friend.

Rockwell gave Collins a break that afternoon. He
asked him to fungo flies to the outfielders while he
handled the infield.

Chip liked to shag flies. What ballplayer doesn't? And
Doc Terring's admonition to refrain from throwing
with his injured right hand was no handicap. Chip
could throw a long ball lefty.

"Here you go, Hilton," Collins called when it was
Chip's turn. "Get on your horse!"

Collins lifted a long, high fly to Chip's right. Chip
tore after it with flying legs, pulled it in with a backhand stab, pivoted on around, thrust the glove under
his right arm, and threw the ball in with his left hand.

The ball came in on a line and Collins nearly dropped the bat.

"You see that?" he called to the fans in the bleachers. "You see that throw? *Left-handed!*"

Jim Collins wasn't the only one who was surprised. The pitchers heard Collins and turned to watch as Chip gathered in another high fly and pegged the ball back with his left hand.

"Show-off!" Byrnes sneered. "More grandstand stuff!"

"I don't think so," Sparks countered. "I think it's great. Wish I could do it! What's he do with the ball when he catches it?"

"Leaves it in the glove," Maxim explained.

Diz Dean demonstrated. "Like this," he said. "He catches the ball in the glove with his left hand, shoves the glove with the ball still in it under his arm, pulls his hand out of the glove, takes the ball out of the glove with his left hand, see? Then he throws the ball with the left hand. I used to play with a one-armed guy. He played the outfield for us. Boy, what a wing!"

"I still say it's grandstand stuff," Byrnes griped. "What reason's Hilton got to throw left-handed?"

"Simple enough," Sparks argued. "He's got a bad right hand. Remember, he's a switch hitter, bats from either side. Why shouldn't he throw lefty if he has the ability? Maybe he's a natural lefty like you are."

"That's right," Joe Maxim added. "I was born a lefty, but my folks changed me to a right-hander. Wish they'd left me alone."

Rockwell broke up the conversation. "All right," he shouted. "Batting practice! Roll that cage up behind the plate, some of you fellows. Infielders do the chasing! Outfielders hit!

"Byrnes, you throw! Nickels and Smith feed the balls.

Let's go! On the double now! Hit three and lay one down and run it out!"

Byrnes didn't like it. Star chuckers frequently get the idea that pitching for batting practice is beneath their dignity. But most good pitchers welcome the opportunity to loosen up, to get the feel of the mound, develop form, and work on the finish of their delivery and fielding position.

Some managers assign their pitchers to batting-practice pitching as a sort of punishment or to eliminate a swelled head. Other managers feel that the risk of injury to a member of the pitching staff, or to a regular player, is too great and prefer to use reserve members of the squad for the chore.

At any rate, Byrnes sullenly and slowly made his way out to the mound. And when he delivered the ball, the result was a halfhearted throw which was of about as much value in developing timing and a hitting eye as playing marbles.

Rockwell, busying himself with the equipment, apparently was unaware of the temperamental southpaw's rebellious attitude. But Rock was still building character. Perhaps reconstructing or repairing is more correct. Anyway, he was still trying to bring the unruly southpaw around, and the practice pitching was a part of the program.

Byrnes continued the indifferent throwing and some of the hitters complained. "Come on, Lefty, throw it as though you meant it."

The plea went unheeded and Rockwell decided to take a hand. "Put a little something on the ball, Byrnes," he called. "Those tosses are a waste of time."

Byrnes mumbled something under his breath and then he began recklessly blazing the ball toward the plate.

Chip was "on deck," swinging a couple of extra bats, and stepped up to the third-base side of the plate when Murph Gillen laid down the bunt and sprinted to first.

Chip had good hitting form. The wide stance and high-poised bat indicated power, and each time he snapped his wrists at the end of the swing, the ball took off like a flash of light, scarcely rising higher than the pitch. But it carried clear to the fence, straight as a string, and the crack of the bat against the ball brought a twist of satisfaction to Chip's lips. The blows brought a spatter of applause from the bleachers, too.

That was the last straw so far as Byrnes was concerned. He frowned grimly as he turned for another ball. Serving them up for anyone was bad enough but it was too much where Chip Hilton was concerned. Byrnes was almost beside himself now. "Waste of time, eh?" he muttered. "Well, watch this, Rockwell!"

Chip knew Byrnes was angry, but there was nothing he could do about it. Right now, he was concerned only with sharpening his hitting eye. He stepped across the plate to the first-base side of the plate for the bunt. He pulled his cap down over his right eye and focused on the delivery.

Chip never had a chance to lay that one down. Byrnes stepped toward first and blazed a sidewinder straight for Chip's head.

"Look out!" Soapy shouted, his voice shrill with alarm. "Look *out!*"

The warning came too late. Chip ducked frantically, dropping the bat and throwing his right arm up protectingly. But fast as he was, the ball was faster. It smacked against his elbow, the crack of the ball against flesh and bone ringing out above the warning shout.

There was a shocked silence and then the players ran to Chip's side. Biggie Cohen and Soapy Smith got there first. "You all right?" they chorused. "You all right, Chip?"

Chip answered with his eyes. He gripped his right elbow with his left hand, scarcely able to stand the agonizing pain which paralyzed his arm. He tried to bend the elbow but the excruciating pain was too much. "Oh, boy," he managed. "Oh, boy!"

# CHAPTER 10

## OUT FOR THE SEASON

DOC TERRING couldn't believe it. "Oh, no!" he cried. "Not again! This is too much! Help him off with that shirt. Easy. Sit up here on the table. Now, what happened?"

"Hit by a wild pitch," Chip explained. "I couldn't get out of the way."

"Wild pitch, my eye!" Soapy exploded. "Byrnes tried to *bean* him!"

Concern flooded Terring's face. "You sure of that?" he asked in a shocked voice.

Soapy nodded emphatically. "I know it!"

"He didn't mean to hit me, Soapy," Chip said, looking at Biggie for support. But Biggie, siding with Soapy, nodded affirmatively.

"Yes, he did!" Soapy insisted. "Biggie heard him and so did I! He said, 'All right, Rockwell, watch this'—or something like that. Right, Biggie?"

"That's right!" Biggie said shortly.

"That doesn't mean he deliberately tried to hit me with the ball," Chip said. "He could have meant a lot of things. Could have meant he was going to strike me out or throw some real hard stuff or most anything."

"He'll get some hard stuff," Soapy threatened. "The first chance—"

Chip checked him. "No, he won't, Soapy. That's out! Besides, this is my party."

"Some party!" Cohen observed bitterly.

All the time this conversation had been going on, Doc Terring gently probed and pressed away at Chip's elbow. "I don't think there's anything broken, Chip," he said, straightening up and rubbing his chin reflectively. "But we'll soon know. We'll take an X ray."

Terring turned to Biggie and Soapy. "You fellows can go on back to practice if you want to. This is going to take about an hour."

"We'd rather wait if you don't mind," Biggie said quietly.

Soapy nodded. "Practice is about over, Doc."

A little later, Red Schwartz, Speed Morris, Flash Sparks, Hutch Kroll, Butcher Durley, and Diz Dean crowded into the room.

"Bad?" Speed asked.

Terring appeared just then and answered the question. "It doesn't look too bad," he said, fastening the damp negative to the glass reflector. "Not bad at all," he said, studying the picture.

"That's a relief," Soapy said thankfully. "Boy, I was worried."

Chip laughed. "*You* were worried! How about me?"

"How about all of us?" Morris demanded.

There was deep silence until Terring turned away from the picture. "Can't see any sort of a break or chip, youngster," he said. "Of course there's a lot of swelling. I'll give you some stuff to take that away and then we'll take another X ray. You'd better sit out practice for a couple of days just to be on the safe side."

Rockwell appeared on the scene in time to hear Terring's diagnosis. "Good," he said. Then he turned to Chip. "How's it, Chipper?"

"Not bad."

Terring nodded. "It looks O.K., Hank. Lucky—" He fashioned a sling and placed it in position. "You wear this until tomorrow afternoon, youngster. Now get out of here. Vamoose! All of you!"

Rockwell and Terring were firm friends and true sportsmen. Each appreciated the responsibilities of the other and they often shared their problems.

"Now what?" Terring demanded.

Rockwell sighed wearily. "Same old thing. Two leaders! Two factions!"

"Too many good ballplayers, maybe," Terring suggested.

"Could be!"

"What happened?"

"Well, it was partly my fault. You know what I've been trying to do with Byrnes. Today I made him pitch to the batters and he couldn't take it. For some reason he's feuding with Chip."

"Jealousy!" Terring said tersely.

"Anyway, he was sulking, and when I told him to put something on the ball, he lost his head and began throwing wild and hit Chip. I don't think the boy is malicious, but it looked as though he didn't care whether he hit Chip or not."

"And?"

"Well, I didn't do anything until after practice. Then I asked him to stop in the office before he showered and I tried to find out what the trouble was."

"Any luck?"

"Not a bit. He clammed up and wouldn't talk. I got nowhere and had to let him go. Then, when I started over here, I saw something that really worries me. Most of the kids were in here, as you know. But Nickels, Gillen, Burke, and Emery were waiting for Byrnes. I don't like it."

"It doesn't look good," Terring admitted.

While Rockwell and Terring were discussing the problem, Byrnes and his crowd were talking about what had happened in Rockwell's office.

"Was he mad?" Emery asked.

Byrnes shrugged. "How do I know? What do I care?"

"Must have been! Wha'd he say?"

"Asked me why I lost my head in the first game and why I was sulking. Lot of junk like that."

"What did you tell him?"

"Didn't tell him anything! Why should I? Had nothing to tell! That is, nothing he'd like very much."

Nick Nickels had been listening to the conversation. He spoke for the first time, just a bit of anxiety in his voice. "You really hit him on purpose, Lefty?"

Byrnes grunted. "Well, maybe not on purpose but—" He hesitated and then continued passionately, "Brother, do I hate that guy!"

Jim Collins stopped by State Drug that evening to see Chip and find out how badly he was hurt. This time, he barged right on back to the storeroom. Chip was pleased by the visit, and Collins left wearing a big smile. Jim was Chip's Number One fan!

After Collins had left, Chip went into a huddle with himself. He was thinking about Lefty Byrnes and Nick Nickels and Emery and Burke and Murph Gillen. Chip figured that it was about time he got straightened out with those five fellows. It had him puzzled. Four were regulars and had no worry about holding their positions. And Lefty Byrnes ranked at the top of the pitching staff. He tried to recall any incident in which he might have offended any of the five. He couldn't remember a single bit of friction.

"Byrnes is the leader, all right," he mused. "No doubt about it. But why is he so bitter?"

Chip was sure of one thing. A pitcher concentrated on the strike zone when he threw a ball; he didn't keep looking at the batter before, during, and after he threw to the plate. He wasn't going to say anything about that to anyone. But he wasn't going to be a fool and get all banged up just because a couple of fellows had it in for him. He could play rough, too—if he had to! The first chance he got he was going to have a straight-from-the-shoulder showdown with Lefty Byrnes.

Henry Rockwell was doing some thinking, too. Rock had exhausted his patience with Lefty Byrnes. He realized that he had jeopardized the baseball career of one of the finest athletes in the country in what appeared to be a vain effort to rehabilitate a spoiled star.

"Yes," Rockwell mused, "I knew all along Byrnes was jealous of Chip, and I let the affair get out of hand. Nickels' return peg might have been deliberate, but I don't think it was malicious. He was probably trying to annoy Chip—not injure him. But Byrnes' bean-ball throw had all the earmarks of an intentional pitch."

At the end, Rockwell had made up his mind that Lefty Byrnes had just about reached the end of his string. The unruly kid was going to get exactly nowhere with the tactics he had been employing. Byrnes was going to "sit" for a game or so, and, if the temperamental southpaw wanted to do a little fretting while he was sitting, that would be all right, too.

Tuesday afternoon, Chip waited impatiently for Doc

Terring. His arm felt much better and a lot of the swelling had disappeared. When Terring arrived, he ushered Chip directly to his private office and carefully examined the elbow. "Coming along nicely, Chip," he said with a pleased smile. "Let's take another picture."

"The first regular game of the season is scheduled for tomorrow afternoon," Chip said suggestively.

Terring's face softened. "I'm sorry, Chip. You'll have to forget baseball for a while."

"But, Doc, my arm feels swell. I—"

Terring checked him. "Chip, you've got years of baseball ahead of you. I know you don't want to risk permanent injury to your arm just for the sake of a little bit of patience. Right?"

Chip's face expressed his disappointment. "I'd just like to keep in shape, Doc. A fellow gets stale if he doesn't work."

Terring smiled understandingly. "I know, Chip. Don't worry, I'll give you the green light just as soon as it's practical for you to work out. O.K.?"

It wasn't O.K., but Chip could do nothing about it. He headed for Jeff with a heavy heart, hoping to get in a little studying before going to work. But he couldn't keep his thoughts away from baseball and soon headed for State Drug. Later, when Soapy checked in for work he told Chip about practice. Nickels had been the only one of Byrnes' pals who had asked how Chip was feeling. But it was Cohen that Soapy wanted to talk about.

"Biggie was fit to be tied, Chip," Soapy said admiringly. "I never saw him like he was today right after practice. We were all dressing and it was sorta quiet and Biggie stood up and rapped on a locker with his spikes and started talking. He said baseball was a fine game, but if fellows couldn't play without pulling mean and dirty tricks, it wasn't worth while.

"Everyone was surprised and there was a little silence you could almost hear. Then Biggie said that if anyone in the room wanted to do any bean-ball throwing or dirty sliding or bat throwing or just plain fighting—he was ready. Boy, you never heard a place so quiet in your life. I never saw Biggie so mad and determined. Even scared *me!*"

Chip sat on the bench for the State Teacher game, but he didn't suit up. Rockwell started Flash Sparks in the box and Soapy behind the plate. Sparks got away to a good start, striking out the first two men he faced and forcing the third to fly to right. Flash was away ahead of the Teacher hitters, far too fast for them.

In the Fence Buster's half, Kroll walked, Morris sacrificed, and Emery banged a double to right. Kroll scored. Cohen looked at a curve and then blasted a hopping fast ball over the right-field fence. That set the fans to yelling "Fence Busters" again. Then Burke accentuated the positive by driving the first pitch deep in left field for a three-bagger. The Teachers called time and sent in another hurler. It didn't help. Durley singled, Murph Gillen punched a double into right center and went on to third when the throw to the plate got away from the Teacher receiver.

That was the way it went all the way. It wasn't much of a ball game but it was action. The fans liked it, and the youngsters gleefully fattened up their batting averages. Rockwell and the Teacher coach agreed to call the game at the end of the fifth. The Fence Busters were on their way and they sent the fans home talking, and won their first regular game of the season 28 to 4.

Rockwell used Sparks for three innings and called on

Silent Joe Maxim for the last two. Soapy caught the entire five innings. Lefty Byrnes and Nick Nickels watched the game from the bull pen.

Chip had arrived at the game with a sling holding his arm; he left with it stuffed in the pocket of his jacket. Chip figured that it might help if his arm got a little exercise.

Terring took another X ray on Thursday and his face was wreathed in smiles when he finished inspecting the negative. He turned to meet Chip's hopeful eyes. "Nothing to worry about now, Chipper. Just a matter of time."

Chip breathed a deep sigh of relief. "Then my arm is all right?"

"Oh, no, I wouldn't say that. But you might be able to start working out in about ten days or thereabouts."

"Ten *days!*"

"That's right. And—"

"But I *can't* wait that long, Doc. Why, there's a game Saturday."

"I know. And there will be another game the following Saturday and the next and the next. There'll be lots of games and lots of Saturdays. Now you listen to me—"

Chip listened. And he sat it out. He sat in the dugout and suffered as only a boy can suffer when he can't play the game he loves.

Rockwell let Byrnes sit, too. He gave him the silent treatment, completely ignoring the southpaw. Byrnes wasn't worried when he was overlooked the first game, but when the second passed, and then the third and he wasn't used, he began to stew. Rock would have found Byrnes' efforts to get attention amusing if he hadn't been so worried about the boy. Byrnes reported early to practice, hustled, talked it up, and nearly tore the glove off of Nickels' hand when he warmed up.

Byrnes got his chance in the Baxter game and the southpaw worked beautifully, getting nine strike-outs and giving up only six scattered hits. The Fence Busters won easily, 18 to 1.

Doc Terring gave Chip the green light on Monday, April 7, and then he broke the bad news. "No throwing with your right arm for four weeks. And no pitching for another two weeks after that."

Chip was demoralized, speechless. "Oh, *no!*" he breathed. "Not for the season?"

# CHAPTER 11

## ONE BAD APPLE

STATE's chief medical officer had more than a professional interest in the university's teams and athletes. He liked sports for sports' sake and he liked youngsters. Terring, Dad Young, Director of Athletics, and Hank Rockwell were close friends. Young had known Rockwell for years and he had been instrumental in bringing the veteran coach to the university. So it was not strange that these three men, so much alike in their approach to sports, should be friends.

Terring was worried about Chip Hilton, not because of the injured elbow, but because of the hurt in the youngster's eyes. It was on his mind to such an extent that he broke an old rule that evening at dinner and surprised Mrs. Terring by talking shop.

"Real tough," Terring said abruptly. "A real tough break."

"What's that, Mike? Someone break a leg or something?"

"No, but I just about broke someone's heart."

"Now, Mike—"

"No, seriously. The Hilton boy. Had to cut off his arm,

104

so to speak, virtually cut out his baseball for a while."

"You mean the youngster who did so well against the varsity?"

"That's the one. Hank's going to be sick when he hears about it. Think I'll call him. Dad, too."

"But your dinner, Mike?"

"Can't eat right now, dear. Sorry! You mind?"

"Of course not."

Henry Rockwell had missed Chip at practice and he had missed Terring on the way home. But he had suspected the worst and was just about to call Terring when the phone rang. It was Terring. Dad Young and he were coming over. Nothing to worry about, just wanted to talk to him.

"Chip?"

"In part," Terring said gently. "Now, don't worry, it's nothing serious."

Dad Young had been at State a long time; he had survived several administrative and athletic changes and was loved by students, faculty, and alumni alike. Young stood by his coaches, realizing that a coach was only as good as his players. He had watched the varsity and frosh in the campus series and had been disgusted with Byrnes' behavior. The information Terring had given him had added to his dislike for the temperamental pitcher.

Rockwell greeted his two friends anxiously. "Chip's arm?" he queried.

"The arm is coming along fine, Hank," Terring assured him. "We just wanted to talk to you about the boy's frame of mind."

"And about a couple of your other players," Young added.

"But what about Chip?"

"He shouldn't do any throwing at all for about four weeks, Hank, and no pitching for a couple more. It will be about six weeks, I'd say, before he'll be able to pitch a game." He made a hopeless gesture. "I'm sorry. But that's only part of it. What I really wanted to talk about was the kid's heart. What I had to tell him today —well, it hurt him a lot. He tried not to show it other than the usual protestations you'd expect from a kid who loves baseball, but he was way down when he left my office."

"Doc and I were wondering if the kid couldn't work out," Young interjected. "Run, shag flies, maybe do a little hitting and running.

"He's a great kid, Hank," Young continued. "Quite a contrast to most of the star athletes we get nowadays. Most of them have been overpublicized and pampered and spoiled until they think the world owes them everything, served on a platter. Chip's never asked the Athletic Department for a thing and I'm sure he could qualify for one of the scholastic or general scholarships. No, he's an independent kid, works and pays his own way. He's the real McCoy."

Rockwell smiled. "You're telling me," he said softly.

"Mike and I have been talking about Byrnes and the player split which has developed," Young went on. "You know, Hank, some boys just aren't worth salvaging. I watched Byrnes in that first game, and if I had been in your shoes, I'd have fired him on the spot. He's a bad apple."

"He must have *some* good qualities, Dad. He's working his way, driving a taxi at nights. A boy can't be really bad who works when he really doesn't have to—"

Young checked him. "Now, just a minute, Hank, let me get this off my chest. Byrnes is the sort of kid who has certain qualities which endow him with a type of leadership that unthinking youngsters sometimes confuse with the real thing.

"In my opinion, the quicker you drop him the better. He's trouble! Now, I've had my say and the rest is up to you."

"But Byrnes has changed," Rockwell insisted. "I think he felt badly about Chip. He's hustled and acted like a different person ever since."

Terring had taken no part in the conversation. He listened quietly, pulling thoughtfully away on his pipe. Now he spoke. "Let me ask you a couple of simple questions, Hank. First, has Byrnes ever said one thing to Chip? Has he ever expressed any regret to the kid he knocked out of baseball?"

Rockwell shook his head. "Why, I don't—"

"Well, I do!" Terring interrupted. "Now, let me answer my own questions. Neither Byrnes nor any of the other four boys in his clique has said a single word to Chip. And, according to all the information I can get, none of the five has ever expressed a bit of regret that the kid can't play. Now you mark my words. As soon as Chip comes back out for that team—as soon as he's able to pitch and starts to pitch the way he can—you'll have trouble with Byrnes again."

"I agree with Mike," Young said firmly. "Byrnes has to be the whole show or he'll break up the act."

The three friends talked for another hour or so, and after Young and Terring departed, Rockwell took off for State Drug. He found Chip in the storeroom, nose in a history book. Rock was only there fifteen minutes, but when he left, Chip's eyes were bright again and he could hardly wait for the next day and practice.

Gee-Gee Gray broke the Hilton story that evening on

his seven-o'clock sportscast. Among the interested listeners was Lefty Byrnes.

"Yes—Hilton was expected back in action this week but Doc Terring put a damper on that—placed the brilliant chucker on the shelf for six weeks.

"Hilton will be missed not only for his pitching but for his prowess with the stick. But his loss—aside from the brilliance of his play—need not be a serious blow. Few, if any, college teams can boast hitters like this freshman fence-busting team. The pitching will be weakened, of course, but the frosh schedule is spaced, and Rockwell has four capable hurlers in Byrnes, Sparks, Dean, and Maxim—"

"Six weeks!" Byrnes exulted. "Now I can make them forget there ever was a guy like Hilton!"

Jim Collins heard the broadcast and hit right out for town to see Chip. He knew how a fellow felt when he got a six-week setback in baseball. He looked at the gnarled fingers of his throwing hand several times on the way. A broken thumb, a forefinger which was still crooked, and enlarged knuckles on all of his fingers attested to the hazards of playing behind the bat.

A lot of Chip's other friends felt the same way Collins felt but hardly knew how to express their sympathy.

"It isn't so bad," Chip told them cheerfully. "Doc Terring said I could work out. After all, I'm lucky not to have a break or a chip."

Byrnes and his crowd were shocked when Chip showed up in the dressing room Tuesday afternoon and suited up for practice.

"Thought he was out for six weeks," Burke said incredulously.

"Probably gonna coach the pitchers," Nickels said mischievously, eying Byrnes.

"Ain't funny," Byrnes growled.

Chip carried on as if nothing had happened during practice, except that he threw or lobbed the ball around with his left hand. He ran the bases and shagged flies and even took a turn in the sliding pit, practicing the hook on his left side, hooking with his right foot, and keeping his right arm out of trouble.

The fans were surprised to see Chip in uniform when they turned out for the Crampton game. The Aggies had a veteran line-up and had won the small college championship the preceding season. Country boys are natural ballplayers and Crampton was located in the farming section of the state.

Rockwell started Silent Joe Maxim and the Fence Busters found out in the top of the very first frame that they weren't going to push the Aggies around. The Aggies teed off on Joe and drove in four runs before the yearlings could get them out. But four runs meant nothing to the Fence Busters and they came hustling in, anxious to get hold of the old willow and punish the ball.

The Crampton chucker was a big, rawboned fellow who simply reared back and gave every pitch everything he had and the heck with what happened thereafter. He was fast and wild.

The Fence Busters were dig-in hitters, who planted themselves solidly in the batter's box and got set to bust the fences. They didn't dig in on the Aggie. Maybe the first time and for the first pitch. After that, they stepped up cautiously, always prepared to duck.

Kroll walked after ducking, twisting, and dodging four weird throws. Hutch had no chance to do anything but walk. Speed Morris was a wonderful hitter for the second position in the batting order, an excellent push-along hitter. But a push-along hitter has to have a chance to lay the wood against the ball or a chance to bunt. Or at least try. Speed didn't have the chance. The chucker was evidently trying to keep them high or inside or both—or maybe he was just inaccurate. At any rate, Speed walked, too.

Bob Emery was a lefty hitter. He stood in the rear of the box and blasted away. He was anxious to maintain his .500 average and swung from the heels at the wild pitches. And the Aggie struck him out!

Biggie Cohen liked the fast ball and that was all the Aggie hurler was throwing. But he was throwing the hard one all over the lot. Biggie ducked and dodged four haphazard throws and landed on first, filling the bases. That brought up Belter Burke and he tried to live up to his nickname, going for the wild pitches. They were all bad, but Belter managed to connect with one he had to hit or get hit, and drove a screamer skipping along the ground to the right of shortstop.

The Aggie infielder made a spectacular stop, smothered the ball, dropped it, picked it up and fired it to second in time to nip Cohen. The throw to first caught Burke for the double play to retire the side. So the Fence Busters took the field without any runs and with just a little bit of apprehension filtering through their cockiness.

The Aggies started right in again and got two tallies before they were retired to lead 6 to 0. And when the Fence Busters came in for their bats in the bottom of the second, the fans were yelling for some runs.

Butcher Durley liked to crowd the plate. The big Aggie fixed that! And quick! He fired a fast one which Butcher couldn't dodge and the ball plunked into Butcher's broad back between the shoulder blades. Rockwell called time.

After making sure that Durley was all right, Rockwell complained bitterly to the umpire about the dangerous pitching. He had a lot of support from the fans. The coach always has the home-town fans behind him in an argument with the visitors.

The Aggie coach came stalking out on the field and wanted to know what was wrong with the "great hitters" he had heard so much about. "Want us to throw underhand, bowl 'em up?" he gibed.

"We don't want to get killed up there," Rockwell retorted.

"Play ball," the umpire ruled. "I don't know whether he knows where the plate is, but I do know he couldn't hit anyone if he tried. Play ball!"

Murph Gillen hit from the first-base side of the plate, but the right fielder didn't hit the Aggie pitcher. The first pitch sent him sprawling in the dust and he never did recover. He struck out on three bad ones and scuffed his way back to the dugout after slinging his bat angrily in that direction.

Nick Nickels was a righty hitter who always settled his two hundred and thirty pounds comfortably in the box and waved a massive bat menacingly at the chucker. He waved it this time, too. Once! That was his last chance. The ball came whistling in and Nick sat down. Fast! After that, the big boy was wary. He thought more about ducking than hitting. But he swung mightily at one of the mad throws, and the result was a high fly which the Aggie second baseman gathered in behind the keystone bag.

Joe Maxim had a lot of courage. The big fellow played tackle in football and moving him was like trying to budge the Rock of Gibraltar. If Silent Joe had been a mite faster on his feet he would have made a fine first baseman or outfielder. Joe pitched righty and batted righty, and he was determined to hit the ball. But Joe was also worried about those six runs and couldn't wait to catch up. He managed to get a piece of a bad ball, popping up to the first baseman for the third out, and the Fence Busters had been blanked two innings in a row for the first time in the young season.

By all rights, the big visiting pitcher should have tired as the game wore on. He should have tired, or begun throwing the ball away, or getting flustered with men on the bases. Or something! But he didn't!

Sparks came in for Maxim in the fourth, but it didn't seem to make much difference to the Aggies. And the further the game went, the more the big, awkward hayseed seemed to like it. He kept smiling and heaving the ball, and the Fence Busters gritted their teeth and tried harder but got nowhere fast.

The frustrated freshmen did manage to blast in two runs in the fifth and three more in the seventh, but the Aggies kept adding to their total, and the tempo of the game remained unchanged. When the visitors took the field for the top of the ninth, they were leading 12 to 5.

The fans were tearing down the stands when the Fence Busters came in for their last at bat. They were cajoling, pleading, demanding some runs. Jim Collins was nearly beside himself and he had yelled himself hoarse. First at the big Aggie chucker, and then in trying to root in some Fence Buster runs.

Morris led off in the bottom of the ninth after a worried look at the scoreboard. Speed had walked twice and the Aggie walked him again. Emery swung at the first pitch; at a ball which was above his head. But some way or other, he hit it, driving the ball far over the spot he himself had scuffed so disgustedly while standing out there throughout the miserable game. Speed scored and Bob pulled up at third.

Then Biggie electrified the crowd by powdering a close ball, pulling it high over the right-field fence. That made it 12 to 8 and gave the Fence Busters life.

The blow brought life to the Fence Buster fans, too. This game wasn't over! The big hayseed pitcher was tiring! The Fence Busters had just been fooling around with the Aggies! Belter and Butcher and Murph would pickle the ball now! Now that the old bats were ringing again!

Burke struck out!

But Durley hit a screamer!

There was a crack, a flash of streaking light toward left field, and a moan from the fans. The Aggie shortstop had leaped high in the air and the ball had stuck in the high-flung glove. Two away!

Gillen hadn't touched the ball all day. Now the fans yelled for a pinch hitter and called on Rockwell to do something. Frantically pleading, demanding, begging him to help the Fence Busters out of this impossible situation.

"Put Hilton in!" a fan behind the dugout yelled in a shrill voice. "He can hit better than that guy with one hand!"

"Hilton," the crowd echoed. "We want Hilton!"

## CHAPTER 12

## DEFENSELESS BUSTERS

ROCKWELL heard the crowd all right. A coach always hears the crowd. And he always hears the cocksure advisers who bellow the moves; call the shots so confidently. But Rockwell didn't intend to put Chip in a spot which might leave him holding the bag. Byrnes and his crowd weren't going to use Chip for any sort of an alibi today. That was all over! The Fence Busters had no one but themselves to blame for this debacle and he didn't intend to let Chip share any part of it. No, Gillen could do his own hitting. Or missing!

Rockwell had no other recourse, really. He couldn't have used Chip in that game under any circumstances. Not until he had let the boy work out a few more days and had proved conclusively to himself that Chip could hit a ball without fear of further injury to his arm.

Murph Gillen heard the fans and cast a questioning look in the direction of third base, but Rockwell turned his back and looked out toward left field. It was too late to do anything now but hit away. Gillen was on his own.

Gillen tried hard. Too hard, maybe. He struck out on

three fireballs! The Fence Busters had lost their first game of the season!

The players didn't waste much time vacating Alumni Field. They left silently and morosely. And there wasn't much talking in the dressing room after the game. Each player seemed in a hurry to get a shower, dress, and get going.

The fans, however, reacted differently. They couldn't seem to realize that the game was over and that the Fence Busters had lost. They moved slowly toward the exits, rehashing the plays and the game.

"That big Aggie didn't have a thing!" someone said angrily.

"Had a lot of speed," another observed.

"Thought the kids liked fast-ball pitching," a hurt voice complained.

"Hitting wasn't so bad," a deep voice contended. "It was the errors in the field that whipped 'em."

A loud-voiced fan summarized the debacle best of all. "Look! They've been trying to bust the fences every time they went to bat. That's their trouble. They believe everything they read in the papers. Think they ought to knock every pitch over the fence. And as far as fielding is concerned, they've *never* played good defensive ball."

Bill Bell must have been listening to the last speaker. The sports editor's Thursday morning *Herald* story laid it on the line in no uncertain terms.

## DEFENSELESS BUSTERS LOSE FIRST OF SEASON
### Frosh Lose to Crampton 12–8

The defenseless Fence Busters lost their first game of the season yesterday afternoon at Alumni Field when Elmer von Schlundt, Crampton's elongated hay baler, wrapped up the bats of the locals and stilled the fence-busting ideas of State's heavy-hitting frosh to lead the Aggies to a 12–8 upset triumph.

If wild swinging and efforts to "kill the ball" are criterions of fence-busting, State's frosh wonders lead the field. Reference to "field" does not imply that Rockwell's freshman phenoms know what the term means on a baseball field. Defense they have none. Pitching they have only when the injured Hilton is on the hill. Power hitting they have when opposing pitchers let them dig in and tee off.

Some chuckers don't let hitters have all the privileges. Elmer von Schlundt belongs in that category. If Henry Rockwell's Defenseless Busters expect to win the Little Four championship they've been driving for they had better forget the fences and start trying to meet the ball. "Nuf sed!"

Wesleyan brings its frosh and varsity teams here Saturday. Game time for the freshman game is 10 o'clock. Varsity game 2:30.

Chip was raring to go when he reported to practice on Thursday. So was Jim Collins. He had taken the responsibility of hitting to the outfielders seriously and had brought his own bat. He was the first person on the field. Chip joined in the shagging of Collins' long flies. But this time there was a difference. Chip was concentrating on his left-handed pegs back to the fan who was taking the return throws. He was pegging them in just the way one would in a game, low and fast and hard and on the first bounce.

The infielders had the first practice licks, and when the outfielders came in for their turn, Rockwell called Chip.

"Arm strong enough for a little hitting, Chip?"

"Feels fine, Coach."

"All right, take a turn."

It was all right. Chip took his turn and met the ball with solid, ringing blows. Rockwell watched the hitting until he was satisfied that Chip could hit the ball without flinching. Diz Dean was chucking the practice throws and he laid them in perfectly for hitting practice.

Chip was driving the ball hard and straight. The ball took off on a straight line, kicking up the dust between the infield and the outfield, skipping hard, clear to the fence. Chip could hit to all parts of the field and switched from the left to the right side of the plate on each of his hitting turns.

The pitchers had been chasing the hits, and when Rockwell sent the outfielders out to "chase," he called for the chuckers to come in and hit. Byrnes waited in the line of Chip's path at second base, fumbling with his shoelace until Chip passed by.

"Faker," Byrnes gritted, keeping his voice low. "Who you think you're fooling about that elbow?"

Chip turned and came back. "I'm not trying to fool anyone about my arm, Byrnes," he said coolly. "I hope you don't think you fooled me when you threw that bean ball."

"Thought you got hit in the arm."

"I did," Chip said evenly. "But you aimed at my head —right?" He looked the ill-natured pitcher directly in the eyes. "That's dirty baseball, Byrnes."

Byrnes shifted his eyes and turned away. But he couldn't resist one last barb. "Rockwell's grandstander," he hissed. "Hard to be a star with a bum arm, isn't it, grandstander?"

Chip was tempted to follow Byrnes, to force a showdown right then and there. But he didn't want to attract the attention of his teammates and start a rhubarb on the diamond, so he continued on to the outfield. He tried to figure it out for the thousandth time. What was it all about? This feud had gone far enough! He'd have a face-to-face talk with Lefty Byrnes the first chance he got! The sooner the better! He'd show Byrnes about the "bum arm" too. Soon!

Chip really leveled off on Friday. He was feeling right and got a bit further under the ball, sending it far and high, often over the fence. Right then he opened the eyes of his teammates with his power hitting. Except for Rockwell and his high school buddies, his frosh teammates hadn't seen Chip really put the wood to the ball. Chip had decided to go all out. He had held back as long as he could. Hurt and puzzled by the injustice of the whole thing, Chip was now fully determined to be the best ballplayer on the field. He laced the ball with all the smoothness, timing, and power at his command.

Biggie Cohen and Nick Nickels had more weight, but they lacked the smoothness and wrist snap which enabled Chip to flash his bat through at the last instant and to give the wood the all-important last-second impetus which increases the speed of the willow to and through the ball.

The Wesleyan frosh arrived in town Friday night and some of the players drifted into State Drug. One of the fellows recognized Chip and spoke to him. "Playing baseball, Hilton?"

"Got a bum arm. Glad to see you fellows down here. Hear you have a good ball club."

"I heard the same about you," one of the boys retorted. "Been hearing a lot about the Fence Busters. Talk of the state!"

"Last time we saw you was in a basketball uniform," the other boy volunteered. "The night you knocked us out of the tournament."

Chip nodded. "We had a good team. Don't forget you gave us a licking here."

"Yeah, but you didn't play down here. *And* you got twenty-eight points on our floor."

"Anyone can get the points when he gets all the shots," Chip remonstrated.

"Natch!" the taller of the two boys said with a grin. "You playing tomorrow?"

Chip shook his head. "Nope. Wish I were."

The visitors grinned. "Good!" the smaller frosh said. "Maybe we'll win one!"

It was good fun kidding around and Chip liked it. He remembered the basketball trip very well. Wesleyan had been the first of three road games right at the end of the basketball season. All had been "must" games. Loss of one of the three would have eliminated State from the tournament. But they won them all and came back to win the tournament.

Chip hadn't forgotten the hospitality and the friendly spirit of Wesleyan players and students. The game had been bitterly fought, but when it was over, after the defeat had eliminated Wesleyan and kept State in the running, one would never have known Wesleyan had been a contender. No griping, no alibis, no hard feelings. Nothing but praise and good wishes for the winner! That was what sportsmanship was all about. . . .

Jim Collins had been aware of Byrnes' ill-feeling for Chip a long time. He had watched the two boys on the field on Thursday and he had decided to do something about their differences when he noticed the flurry at second base. He didn't have a chance until Friday evening when he surprised Lefty Byrnes as he sat in his taxi on the corner of State and Main.

"Hiya, Lefty. How's business?"

"Good," Byrnes said cheerfully. "Pays for my room and eats, anyway."

"You pitching tomorrow?" Collins asked.

"It's either me or Dean," Byrnes said shortly. "Or at least it should be. Maxim and Dean worked Wednesday."

Collins saw the opening and cleverly took advantage of the opportunity. "Too bad Hilton can't help you fellows out," he said sympathetically. "You need a couple more pitchers. Too many games this early in the season."

Byrnes smiled contemptuously. "Hilton? That grandstander!"

"Grandstander!" Collins echoed. "I never figured Hilton was a grandstander." He studied Byrnes a moment and then said, "Say, just what's wrong with you and Hilton?"

"I'm particular about the kind of fellows I choose for my friends," Byrnes said shortly. "I can't stand the guy."

Collins tried unsuccessfully to get at the source of Byrnes' dislike for Chip. Lefty just wasn't talking about that, and he evaded every leading question. Before he said good night, though, Collins made sure that he left the touchy hurler in a good humor by assuring him that the real fans were pulling for him to come through. The last statement wasn't exactly authentic, but Collins felt that he ought to say something to calm the ruffled chucker.

"Hope the gang gives you better support than they gave the guys Wednesday," he said kindly. "I'll be rooting for you tomorrow, Lefty. Pour it on 'em!"

Byrnes couldn't get Chip Hilton out of his mind that

evening. Surprisingly, in view of his temper, Lefty was a careful driver. That was the reason he was able to take care of his taxi calls and, at the same time, concentrate so deeply on Chip Hilton.

"I don't get it," he kept saying to himself. "Why does everyone rave about Chip Hilton?"

Byrnes was trying to justify his jealousy of Chip Hilton. He assured himself that a fellow had to stand up for his rights even if he had to take on the coach and the whole team. Byrnes had to admit that Chip could hit a baseball and he guessed that Rockwell's pet had something on the ball as a pitcher, but why all the raves? Byrnes guessed further that it must be left over from the football and the basketball seasons. He'd never been much of a football or a basketball player himself and maybe that had been a mistake. Byrnes just couldn't understand baseball fans. "Hilton comes in and gets some breaks and then meets a ball just right and wins a game and they think he's the greatest since Christy Mathewson."

A little later Byrnes spotted Nickels and Gillen and took them for a ride. He told them about Collins' visit and the conversation about Chip Hilton. "Said we ought to be friends," Byrnes said, laughing derisively. "Imagine that!"

"Nice guy, Collins," Nickels said thoughtfully. "Sure been nice to us. I like him."

Gillen nodded. "Goes double for me. Jim's a real nice guy."

Rockwell and Terring spent the evening at the Young residence. Rockwell was full of the good news about Chip's arm. The casual observer would never have known the extent of the deep respect and love the veteran mentor held for Chip Hilton. It was never apparent in his treatment of the youngster on the ball field. But Rock couldn't fool his two friends. They realized the bond which existed between the two and appreciated the veteran mentor's interest in the young athlete.

"He's really banging the ball in hitting practice," Rockwell enthused. "I've always thought Chip would be more valuable to a team as an outfielder than as a pitcher. In fact, he played first base for me one season and worked behind the plate the next. Powdered the ball both years."

"He's some pinch hitter," Terring added. "Jeeps, he *always* comes through!"

Rockwell started out for Alumni Field the next morning fully determined to use Chip if the opportunity presented itself. Before the game he thought it might be wise to prepare the Fence Busters for the worst and he held a short pre-game skull session. He laid the cards on the table right off the bat.

"I thought our line-up was pretty well set," Rockwell began, looking from player to player. He hesitated long enough for that to sink in and then continued. "But we've lost sight of a lot of the things we worked on before the season started. We've been reading all the newspaper twaddle about being sluggers and, worse, believing it! Time and again I've stressed the importance of stroking the ball, meeting the pitch with a smooth swing, and letting the distance take care of itself. But the second you fellows throw away the extra bats and reach the plate you begin aiming for the fences.

"I want you to go out there this morning and prove that you are thinking in terms of the team and not personal batting averages and home runs. If you don't—"

There was a long, tense pause before Rockwell continued. "If you don't, I'll have to make some changes. That's all. Byrnes will pitch, Nickels catch. Let's go!"

The Fence Busters tried hard to play team baseball that afternoon. They used all the inside baseball they had been taught; the advance plays and the bunt and the steal and the squeeze. And they tried to forget the fences. But you don't cure bad habits as easily as you toss away the resin bag.

No, you have to use your signs and employ your "inside" baseball in the games until they become a part of your regular play. The Fence Busters hadn't tried to do anything in the games so far except knock down the fences. So they messed everything up.

Byrnes worked hard but his support was bad and Wesleyan got the lead and held it. As the innings rolled by and the visitors stayed out in front, Byrnes grew garrulous and bitter. His teammates didn't give him the support his pitching deserved and they didn't hit. It wasn't until the bottom of the eighth, with two down and Wesleyan leading 8 to 5, that the Fence Busters got going.

Cohen walked. Belter Burke smashed a hard grass-cutter along the third-base line, which the visitors' hot-corner guardian barely managed to knock down, the ball spinning away from his glove. Cohen hit the dirt at second and beat the throw. Burke fairly flew down to first, his long legs eating up the ninety feet as if it were sixty. Both were safe.

The fans had long since stopped their futile demands for Chip Hilton when Rockwell electrified them by choosing this spot to use Chip as a pinch hitter. They greeted the decision with a tremendous cheer.

The Wesleyan chucker was a righty and Chip stepped

into the first-base side of the batter's box. He worked
the count to two and two and then met a letter-high
curve ball right on the nose. Chip pulled the hook just
enough to give him lots of power, and the ball took off
over the center fielder's head and over the fence. The
fans cheered him every step of the 360 feet around the
bases.

That tied up the ball game 8 to 8, and Nick Nickels
proved that there was still a lot of power left in the
State bats by poling the first pitch far over the left-field
fence. The Fence Busters were ahead for the first time
in the game 9 to 8. Byrnes struck out and Rockwell sent
Red Schwartz out to right field in place of Chip and
started the home-run hitter for the dressing room.

Byrnes seemed to take heart once he was out in front
and, in the top of the ninth, blazed them in, striking
out the first hitter on four pitches. The second batter,
the visitors' peppy second sacker and lead-off man,
worked the count to three and one and then dropped
a surprise bunt in front of the plate which caught Nickels napping. The little scooter was well up the base
path before Nick fielded the ball. Nickels threw before
he was set and the ball sailed high over Cohen's head
and on out into the right-field corner.

Red Schwartz had backed up the play and fielded the
ball as fast as he could, but the little runner had scurried around second before Red grasped the ball.
Schwartz made a fine throw to third, but the runner
slid into the bag ten feet ahead of the peg. Byrnes went
dead white and glared at Nickels with frustrated fury.
For a brief second it appeared that he was on the verge
of duplicating his previous display of temper. But he
managed to control himself with a tremendous effort
and faced the plate.

The next batter was the push-along hitter and he promptly laid down a perfect placement to the right of the mound. The third-base runner was in with the tying run almost before Byrnes touched the ball. Then, to make it worse, Byrnes' throw to first was in the ground and Biggie Cohen's long stretch was of no avail as the bunt expert beat the pickup by half a step. That brought up Wesleyan's long-ball hitters.

The Number Three hitter followed the push-along batter's example and tapped the one-and-no pitch to the right of the mound. Byrnes fielded it perfectly but his hurried throw to second was wild and both runners were safe.

That did it! Blind with fury, Byrnes threw his glove to the ground and jumped on it. Rockwell called time and hurried out to the mound, motioning for Sparks on the way.

"Too bad, Byrnes," Rockwell said shortly. "You worked a good game. Hit the showers."

Byrnes mouthed something and slouched away, too angry to care about the boos from the crowd. But he got a surprise. The fans hesitated a brief moment and then gave him a solid round of applause. That appeased the angry chucker for a second, but when he reached the third-base bleachers, his head was down and he was burning with humiliation and rage. He didn't look up until he reached the left-field gate and almost bumped into Chip Hilton.

# CHAPTER 13

## TWO IN A POD

LEFTY BYRNES and Chip Hilton were almost "two in a pod." Byrnes was an inch taller and five pounds heavier but his drooping posture evened the height, and the difference between a hundred and eighty-five and a hundred and ninety pounds is hardly noticeable. The two boys stood there eying each other without a word for a long moment. Byrnes because he was caught by surprise; Chip because he wanted Byrnes to make the first move.

Byrnes was the first to speak. "Get out of my way, grandstander," he snarled. "We had a winning ball club until you sucked your way back into uniform with your sympathy act."

"How many games did *you* win?" Chip asked softly.

Byrnes' face flooded with anger and, without warning, he started a vicious hook for Chip's jaw. Chip knocked the left-hand lead aside easily and swung in behind the raging southpaw. Then he clamped his left arm around Byrnes' neck and turned his body sharply to the right, tripping the lefty's body with his thigh. Byrnes fell heavily to the ground but he was up almost as soon as he had landed. He was up and rushing at Chip with angry imprecations, swinging wildly.

Byrnes was easy pickings for Chip. The southpaw was a clumsy fighter. He knew nothing about boxing, swung with all his strength and telegraphed every punch. Chip didn't attempt to hit the reckless Byrnes. He simply slapped and tapped his opponent as he rolled with the punches or ducked the wild blows. Breathing heavily, Lefty suddenly realized that Chip was toying with him. He stopped short and dropped his hands, frustrated and almost speechless.

"Why don't you stand up— Stand up and fight?" he managed.

Chip smiled and shook his head. "You don't know how to fight, Byrnes. Besides, there's nothing to fight about. I had hoped we could talk this thing over— whatever it is! I have no idea what I did to get you sore at me and I'd like to know what it's all about."

For a second, Chip thought Byrnes was going to rush him again. But the angry chucker dropped his eyes and turned away without answering. There was something pitiable about Byrnes' sudden deflation and Chip felt sorry for the boy.

"If I've ever hurt you in any way, Byrnes," Chip said softly, "I'm sorry."

Byrnes made no reply, continuing on toward the gym, head bowed, legs lagging, his whole carriage expressing defeat. Chip turned back to see what had happened in the game.

Nothing good had happened. Sparks had forced the first batter to pop up, an infield fly which made it two down with runners still on first and second. The Wesleyan catcher, hitting fifth in the batting order, had a good eye and had tagged the ball hard in his previous trips to the plate. Rockwell signaled for the intentional pass. That filled the bases and brought up the visitors' right fielder. The fellow had struck out twice and grounded weakly to second base, and it was good baseball to pass the heavy hitter to get at him. But this time he really tagged the ball. Swinging wildly at one of Sparks' fast balls, the hitter blasted the ball over the right-field fence and Wesleyan was ahead 12 to 9. Flash got the next batter on a high fly.

With the heavy end of the Fence Busters batting order up in the bottom of the ninth, the fans took heart. But Kroll was thrown out on a hard grounder to short, Morris lined a long fly to left field for the second out, and Bob Emery went down swinging. The Fence Busters had lost two in a row!

Byrnes had showered and was dressing when Chip reached the dressing room. There was no one else in the room but neither boy spoke. The silence was heavy but not filled with the antagonism one might have expected. It was an uneasy, awkward silence, one which speech would have jarred one way or another. Byrnes didn't look up but kept his head lowered, his whole attitude one of despair.

Chip cast one hasty glance at the dejected boy and hurried into the shower, wishing he could do something, just anything to cheer up the disheartened chucker. Chip had been thinking about Byrnes all the way up the hill. All rancor had left Chip with Byrnes' sudden collapse. In fact, he felt genuinely sorry for Lefty. "There's something behind all this," Chip reflected. "Something that happened a long time ago and I had nothing to do with it. If it wasn't me, it would be someone else. What in the world is he trying to prove?"

Moments later, the Fence Busters came clattering

in, their spirits far from keeping time to the happy-go-lucky clackety-clack of their spikes. State's frosh sensations were as low as a bunch of ballplayers always are when victory has been snatched from their grasp.

Rockwell didn't do much talking Monday and Tuesday, but he had everyone hustling. McGuire took turns with Bob Emery in center field, and Red Schwartz alternated with Murph Gillen in right. Eddie Anderson nearly jumped out of his shirt when Rockwell gave him a long workout at shortstop. Bebop Leopoulos and Junior Roberts were butter-fingered and shocked silly when they worked out on the first team.

The regulars started the game at Midland Prep and lasted until the eighth. Then Rockwell made his wholesale substitutions. Chip had batted for Emery in the top of the seventh and had batted in two runs on a triple to deep right center. But he died on third and was replaced by Leopoulos when State took the field. The Fence Busters finished the game with a line-up the home-town fans would never have recognized and came back to the campus smarting and completely demoralized after three straight defeats.

The benched regulars came out Thursday expecting the worst and got it. Got it straight from the shoulder. Rockwell kept his reserves in the line-up.

Saturday brought a big turnout for the Southeastern game. Most of the faithful fans turned out early, determined to find out what had happened to the Fence Busters. But they didn't have a chance to analyze the regulars. Rockwell started his revamped line-up. The reserves were short on talent, but they hustled! Silent Joe Maxim worked his head off, bearing down on every pitch.

The Fence Busters got behind in the third, Southeastern taking a 6–3 lead. In the seventh, with no one out, Schwartz beat out a slow roller to short. Durley hit behind Schwartz and the ball slipped through the hole into right field. Schwartz tore on around to third and Durley reached second. Then Rockwell sent Chip in to hit for Junior Roberts.

Chip got a big hand from the stands, but the applause had scarcely slackened when he blasted a fast ball over the center-field fence. It was a terrific smash and the blow carried all of Chip's pent-up determination and power. The three-run home run tied up the game and that was the score when the Fence Busters took the field in the top of the eighth.

The fans had cheered Chip to the skies for the home run but they nearly tore down the stands when they saw him trotting out to right field.

"Things will be different now," Jim Collins shouted, his face wreathed in smiles for the first time in days.

"How's he gonna throw?" a fan demanded. "What's he gonna do when there's runners on base?"

"He'll peg it!" Collins barked. "He can peg the ball a mile left-handed."

"So can I," someone chortled. "From a plane!"

"He doesn't need a plane," Collins retorted. "I've seen him throw. You wait!"

They didn't have long to wait. Maxim walked the first hitter and hit the next. Then the Southeastern cleanup batter connected and drove the ball high in the air clear to the right-field fence. Chip high-tailed back and waited. The runners waited, too—tagged up and waited for the catch. The fans were standing, watching the drama of this tense situation.

The ball seemed to come off the fence but Chip gathered it in and began his transfer of glove and ball to his right armpit. The base runners had sprinted with the catch, and the third-base coach had waved the first visitor on around third and toward home. Then Chip pegged the ball!

The fans watched with unbelieving eyes as the ball came in on a low trajectory, straight as a string for the plate. There was no cutoff on the throw. Not on that one! Everyone in the park could see that the ball was coming in to home plate with a perfect bounce and that it had the runner by twenty feet. Everyone but the runner himself. He came on, sure of the score, until Soapy took the low bounce and tagged him out.

The fans were still yelling when Soapy fired the ball down to third base. The second runner tried a hook slide and Eddie Anderson tagged him out. It was great baseball and the stands buzzed.

"What a throw! And left-handed!"

"Clear from the fence on the first bounce! Came in like a shot!"

"Wouldn't have believed it if I hadn't seen it!"

"What a guy! Hits from both sides of the plate and throws with either hand!"

"What's that coach thinking about? That kid oughta be some place in the line-up every game."

"Yeah, some place or any place! Don't make any difference to him!"

Up in the broadcasting booth, Gee-Gee Gray had been sputtering all over the place. Gee-Gee couldn't find words to explain the throw. He had been talking about Chip, second-guessing Rockwell. Doubting the wisdom of playing a boy in the outfield who couldn't throw.

"—And—and straight as your clothesline after a hard rain—right to the plate on the first bounce. Honest!

And it had the runner a mile. I've seen everything now —this kid hits the ball out of the park—bats from either side of the plate—throws with either hand— pitches no-hitters— Excuse me, fans, your old pal is out of words. Plumb clean and empty out of words and adjectives."

Chip's throw to the plate and Soapy's blazing peg to third base broke the visitors' backs. The next hitter struck out and the score held at 6 to 6 right down to the last hitter of the game—Chip Hilton!

The Southeastern coach didn't give Chip a chance to be the hero this time. He ordered an intentional pass. Rockwell called time and sent Nick Nickels up to the plate to bat for Soapy Smith.

Chip danced off first base, teasing the chucker. It looked as if he was faking, but he went right down on the first throw, a pitchout. The catcher had called the pitch in self-protection, but he didn't really believe Chip was going. Not on the first pitch. But he was ready and his throw was hard and fast and on the first-base side of the bag. But it was high. Chip slid in on the inside, his right toe hooking the bag and his body falling away toward the pitcher, his right elbow protected. It was fast and beautiful and he was safe!

Gee-Gee Gray quit on that one. He simply told his listeners that he gave up and that they'd have to read about this one-man ball club in the papers.

It was up to Nickels, now. Chip had gotten him ahead of the pitcher and was all set to score. Any kind of a hit would bring him in. Chip kept one foot on the bag, breathing heavily and waited for the hit. The pitcher checked up on him, went into his stretch, lowered his hands and checked again. Chip didn't move. But the steal had unnerved the chucker and he missed the plate. Before the next pitch, he checked Chip again.

Chip was standing by the bag, seemingly satisfied, seemingly waiting for the hit.

Rockwell gave Nickels the "take" sign and the pitcher must have guessed it, for he laid a perfect strike right across the middle of the plate. The catcher grinned and tossed the ball back with an encouraging "Atta baby!"

Then Chip moved!

To the amazement of everyone, Chip lit out for third base, sprinting madly for the bag. The startled pitcher was absorbed in the hitter; he heard the frantic shouts of his teammates too late. But he whirled and threw the ball, a wild peg which nearly got away from the third baseman. Chip was in with a straight slide, and the crowd went wild.

When the cheers died down there were a lot of second-guessers who decried the play, bemoaning the dire possibilities of what might have happened.

"It was a bad play!"

"Coulda lost the game!"

"Isn't any better on third than he was on second!"

"Bet the coach didn't call that play! Not with two down!"

The last two fans were wrong on both counts. Rockwell had called the play and a runner is always better off on third than on second. Rockwell knew how Chip could run bases, and he took the responsibility for the decision.

The pitcher was rattled now. So was the catcher. Chip charged down the base line with every pitch, threatening the steal. The count went to three and one. Then the chucker gave up and threw an intentional walk ball and Nickels trotted down to first. Hutch Kroll hadn't hit all day and Rockwell sent Speed Morris up to bat in his place.

The chucker was all the way up in the air, now. He

kept throwing to third and watching Chip and worrying. On the two-and-one pitch, Chip did it! He broke for home! And he beat the throw!

That broke up the ball game and the fans nearly tore down the stands. They came spilling out on the field and surrounded Chip and his happy teammates.

## CHAPTER 14

## RHUBARB CLIMAX

BIGGIE COHEN, Red Schwartz, and Speed Morris walked slowly toward Jeff, rehashing the game and talking about Chip's base running.

"What's with Chip?" Schwartz demanded. "He's playing like a crazy man!"

"Sure is," Speed agreed. "I never saw him like this! Never saw him so determined to play."

Biggie shook his head. "He shouldn't be playing," he said abruptly. "I'm surprised at Rock."

"You know Chip." Speed grinned. "He'd play if he had to crawl, especially since Byrnes and his crowd got smart."

"Gave me a pep talk last night," Schwartz said ruefully. "Told me I oughta be playing regular."

Strange as it may seem, Chip was thinking about Red Schwartz at that very moment. One would have thought that Chip would be reviewing the game, basking in the thrill of being the star in a great victory. But Chip never spent much time looking over his shoulder. Right now, he was planning a surprise for the troublemakers and Red Schwartz was important in his plans. Chip

135

was determined to show Byrnes and Company that they weren't the only freshman ballplayers on the State campus.

"Red's a good outfielder," Chip murmured, "and he can hit! I'll give it to him tonight again!"

Fireball Finley was the first person Chip saw when he arrived at State Drug and that gave him another idea. "Fireball," he whispered jubilantly. "Just the ticket! Another outfielder. Just what we need."

Then Chip did something he had never done since he first began to work for George Grayson. Without thinking of the consequences, he reacted just as he would have moved to make a play on the diamond; he made a sudden decision. He stopped in front of the cashier's desk and smiled at Mitzi Savrill.

Mitzi was so surprised she almost forgot to turn on the charm. But Mitzi recovered quickly. Mitzi was like that. "I heard about it, Chip. Congratulations. The boss said you were great!"

"I didn't know Mr. Grayson liked baseball."

"Well, he isn't too fond of the game except when one of the staff is playing," Mitzi said archly.

"He ought to see that Fireball comes out for the team, then."

"Why?"

"Because Fireball was one of the best high school players in the country. And because the team's not going too well and we need him."

Mitzi nodded thoughtfully. "Isn't that a gold baseball Cynthia Ann Collins is wearing?"

Chip nodded. "Sure. How'd you know she was wearing a gold baseball?"

"Women dress for women, Chip."

"Not Cynthia! She dresses for Fireball. They've got it bad!"

"Er—most girls get their boy friend's trophies, don't they?"

Chip debated. "Well, I guess so. But—"

"Never mind, Chip. You know, I was just thinking that if you had a gold baseball like that— I mean one you could spare. Why, ahem! I think I might be able to do something about Mr. Grayson and Fireball and baseball."

Chip's smile vanished. He might have known, he told himself. He might have known Mitzi would trip him up someway. He had a gold baseball, all right, but he hadn't figured on giving it to Mitzi Savrill . . . or any other girl. Then he thought of Byrnes and Rock and the Little Four championship and that did it.

"O.K.," Chip said lamely. "It's a deal."

Mitzi smiled. "That's all right, Chip," she said softly. "I never wear jewelry. Thanks, anyway."

Chip's ears were a bright red when he passed the fountain. He didn't glance at Fireball Finley but he heard the little cough and the knowing chuckle. He was in for it now.

Mitzi Savrill was in deep thought the next morning when George Grayson walked past the cashier's desk. And for the first time as long as he could remember, Mitzi's cheery, "Good morning, Mr. Grayson," was lost in a faraway look.

Halfway back to the office, Grayson's steps slowed and he turned back. Mitzi was an important cog in the operation of State Drug, and George Grayson was concerned about anything which disturbed Mitzi. He stood quietly in front of the counter studying the girl. Such concentration was unusual, something was seriously wrong. He tapped gently on the counter. "Why all the deep blue?"

Mitzi started. Her eyes flashed wide in surprise.

"Why, Mr. Grayson, you scared me out of my wits."

"Yes?"

"I mean it!"

"I'm sorry, but why the brown study?"

"Frankly, I'm worried about the drop in our fountain business."

"I've noticed it, but what can be done about that? It's spring, Mitzi."

"All the more reason to be worried. This should be the biggest time of the year for fountain business."

"Well, what's the answer?"

"It's simple. Go back to the principle which made your fountain the campus center in the first place. Go back to star athletes."

Grayson smiled and waved at the cigar counter, candies, magazines, and trinkets which surrounded Mitzi. "Don't think I need that kind of an attraction. There isn't another store in town with a bigger cashier business."

"Why, Mr. Grayson! Now I *am* surprised. I thought you knew that women spent eighty percent of the nation's income."

Grayson grinned wryly. "Ummm. So?"

"College girls like sports stars."

"Looks like we've got a corner on that department with Hilton and Smith."

"But, Mr. Grayson, how about Finley? Why, he was All-State and the big-league scouts all chased him. Why not have *three* baseball stars on the pay roll?"

"What's this supposed to be, the State Athletic Department?"

"No, just the biggest sports center in town. And it ought to be kept that way. Johnny can fill in until the rush hour, because there's not enough sandwich business to keep both him and Bill Porter busy. It looks bad when the help isn't hustling."

Grayson threw up his hands. "Hold everything," he said defensively. "You *win!* Just what do you want me to do?" His voice was harsh and distraught, but he was grinning. He was still grinning when he climbed the steps to his office.

Chip usually took it easy on Sundays except for church and his books. But not this Sunday. He sought out his Valley Falls buddies and Eddie Anderson and Junior Roberts and Bebop Leopoulos, and laced into all of them about the way they were playing ball.

"No one has a job cinched," Chip said aggressively. "You know that! Rock will play the best man no matter whether it's the first game or the last. And don't tell me anything about having to be twice as good as the other fellow. I know that as well as you do. Come on! Let's start tomorrow afternoon!"

Soapy summed it up when Chip retired to do some studying. "Seems to me it's pretty important to someone else," he said significantly. "Guess some of the Fence Busters are in for a surprise. Anyway, I know one five-cent guy who's in for some amay—amase— amazement."

Biggie snickered. "A nickel's worth?"

"Yeah, a Nick Nickel's worth!" Soapy retorted.

Fireball Finley got the surprise of his life Monday morning when he received an urgent call from George Grayson. He got another when Grayson advised him that he had heard about his baseball playing and he'd like it very much if Fireball would report for the team that afternoon—and *"make it!"*

A lot of people were surprised that afternoon. Fireball surprised Rockwell by reporting and squelching any and all doubt about his baseball ability by smashing the ball all over the lot and over the fences. His timing was off but his performance was enough to prove that he knew what to do with the willow.

In the outfield, Fireball gobbled in everything Jim Collins hit anywhere near him. That nearly floored Collins. He hadn't even known Finley played baseball. Finley was fast. He had proved that in football. Collins' daughter could have told him all about Fireball, but she preferred to let her father form his own opinions about her friends. Anyway, Chip and Rockwell were two of the few who knew that Fireball could run the length of a football field in full uniform in a little over ten seconds.

Chip was tickled pink but no one would have known it from the expression on his face. He hustled grimly every second and every time Red Schwartz glanced at his buddy he got a big scowl. That was enough for Schwartz. He caught fire and surprised Rockwell and everyone else by moving into Belter Burke's left-field position during practice and demonstrating that he was a determined candidate for the outfielder's job. Soapy was never better with the stick and behind the plate.

It was a surprising afternoon. Eddie Anderson looked like a million dollars at shortstop, and Speed Morris, who had been at that position since the first day of practice, sobered immediately. Bebop Leopoulos, Fireball Finley, Red Schwartz, Junior Roberts, and Chip played like demons in the outfield.

Belter Burke, Bob Emery, Murph Gillen, and Nick Nickels all were nursing bad tempers when practice ended. Lefty Byrnes didn't have to lead the griping that afternoon.

"What goes?" Burke demanded. "What's got into those guys?"

"What do *you* think?" Emery retorted. "Hilton's been working on the coach. Anyone can see that! Finley works at State Drug, doesn't he?"

"Could be," Burke said thoughtfully. "Whaddaya think, Lefty?"

"I don't know," Byrnes said shortly.

Nickels and Gillen said nothing. Nick Nickels was beginning to doubt that he really was the Number One catcher on the Fence Busters, and Gillen was thinking that Chip Hilton was hitting and fielding too good for him to be sure of his right-field job.

Lefty Byrnes was strangely quiet. Lefty was trying to analyze his feelings toward Chip Hilton. He was disturbed by his reaction in the rhubarb following the Southeastern game. He couldn't understand why he had quit. Byrnes was no coward and his hatred toward Chip Hilton was deep-seated. But the desire to fight Hilton had disintegrated almost as soon as he realized that Chip had no desire to hurt him. It's hard to fight a fellow who tries to reason with you while he is demonstrating that he can whip you with one hand tied behind his back.

Byrnes was thinking about Chip's footwork and his clever boxing. He could feel a red glow of embarrassment creeping up the back of his neck and into his face as he thought of his wild blows and clumsy efforts. "Acted almost like he was handling a baby," he muttered.

Nickels looked at him curiously. "What did you say, Lefty?"

Byrnes made no reply. Nickels and the others exchanged puzzled glances. This wasn't the Lefty Byrnes they had grown to know. Other times and days like this, Lefty had lashed out bitterly at the mere mention of Chip Hilton's name. Everything seemed out of focus all at once. Each of the boys loved baseball and each suddenly realized that he might have a fight on his hands to stay on the team.

They found out Wednesday afternoon after the short bus ride to Slatesville. Rockwell called out the batting order in the dressing room and they suddenly knew that they had a real fight on their hands.

"We'll hit this way," Rockwell said briskly. "Kroll, second base; Anderson, shortstop; Finley, center field; Cohen, first base; Hilton, right field; Durley, third base; Schwartz, left field; Smith, catch; Maxim, pitch. Let's go!"

Rockwell was giving the hustlers a chance and it paid off. The Fence Busters didn't ruin the Slatesville outfield fences, but they did play smart baseball and won 9 to 2. Chip had three for four, and Fireball had two for three, one of them a home run in the fourth with Kroll aboard to break the 2–2 tie. Joe Maxim went all the way and looked stronger in the bottom of the ninth than in the first.

So, the Fence Busters chalked up their second victory in a row without the griping sluggers.

Most of the squad joined in the happy singing on the way home in the bus. But not Byrnes, Nickels, Gillen, Burke, and Emery. They were inwardly boiling with jealousy and futility, and bitter in their silence. And when they showed up at practice on Thursday, the sloppiness of their play and their "don't-care" attitude was so obvious that the rest of the players could actually feel the tension building up. Rockwell sensed the crisis and was ready for the showdown.

Matters came to a head when Rockwell told Byrnes to pitch for batting practice. "You throw to the hitters, Byrnes," he said easily. "Nickels, you catch."

"I'm pretty wild, Coach," Byrnes gritted. "I might hit one of the regulars."

"That's right, Byrnes," Rockwell agreed, smiling blandly. "On second thought, you'd better chase a few flies. Do you good to do a little running."

"Sure been sitting enough," Byrnes muttered. "Half the night in a taxi, most of the day in school, and all the time on the bench."

"A little rest doesn't hurt a hard-working chucker."

"Driving a taxi nights and going to school and playing baseball isn't easy. And keeping eligible, too."

"I realize that, Lefty."

"I thought maybe you felt a fellow who drove a taxi didn't rate. Wasn't good enough. Thought maybe I ought to turn in my suit."

There was a heavy silence. It seemed almost as though the other players had overheard the conversation and had checked their chatter to listen. It wasn't true, of course, but the shouts and practice noise did seem to quiet down at that moment. Undoubtedly because every player on the field sensed what was taking place.

Rockwell took his time making a reply. He studied the trademark on the ball he was holding, delaying an answer. Finally he began to talk. "That wasn't fair, Byrnes. Any boy who works his way through school is to be admired. I was speaking only about baseball. You see, Lefty, it was my belief that you loved baseball and came to State with the idea of getting an education and playing ball at the same time and that you were looking ahead to big-league baseball. If your studies are suffering because of the time you devote to baseball—well, you ought to drop out."

Rockwell paused. Then, tossing the ball in the air

and catching it with the same hand a number of times, he continued. "You know, Byrnes," he said softly, "if every boy who tried out for baseball made the team there wouldn't be much glory in wearing a uniform. Some players have to sit on the bench and hope and work and practice until their opportunity comes.

"The good players have to sit, too, once in a while. Have to be big enough to realize that the other fellow has a right to be given an opportunity to star."

Rockwell's voice was hard and serious as he continued. "You're a fine pitcher, Byrnes. You've got all the tools of the trade. But you're never going to be a great pitcher, the truly great pitcher you can be, until you develop emotional balance, learn to control your temper. I hope—"

Rockwell didn't have a chance to finish the sentence. At least not in Byrnes' presence. Lefty pivoted quickly away without a word and headed for the gate. Over by the plate, Nick Nickels watched his pal stride away. Then, hesitating momentarily, he laid the catcher's glove on the ground and removed the chest protector and shin guards. Although there was no halt in the practice, there wasn't a boy on the field who didn't know that Nick had handed the equipment to Soapy Smith and had followed his friend.

Emery, Gillen, and Burke were chasing flies, but they saw Byrnes and Nickels leave. They didn't say anything and they made no move to follow, but if one had made the break, the others would have fallen in line.

Soapy and Diz Dean took over for the hitters and the workout went on as if nothing had happened. But every player realized that the rhubarb which had been brewing all season had reached the climax.

# CHAPTER 15

## HUSTLE PAYS OFF

BAD NEWS travels fast and the practice incident became a choice bit of gossip for every fan in town. Jim Collins heard about it shortly after supper and decided he'd do something about it right off the bat. That was the reason he waited at State and Main until nearly nine o'clock. Collins wanted to have a little talk with Lefty Byrnes. He was in luck. Byrnes appeared with the taxi loaded down with Nickels, Burke, Gillen, and Emery. Lefty braked the taxi to a brisk stop and backed into the taxi stall. Murph Gillen was talking and the occupants of the taxi were so intent on what he was saying that Collins waited quietly.

"Nope," Gillen said stubbornly, "I can't. I can't quit! Not when Hilton's going so good."

"What's that got to do with it?" Burke demanded.

"Plenty! He's playing better ball than I ever did in my life. Why, if I quit now, everybody in school will say I can't take it."

That remark chilled Gillen's four listeners and checked the conversation. After a short silence, Nick

145

Nickels stirred restlessly and cleared his throat. "You think we're doing the right thing?" he asked, addressing no one directly but glancing at Byrnes out of the corner of his eye.

Lefty Byrnes wrenched the hand brake all the way back. "No one asked *you* to walk out," he said hotly. "Do as you please!"

Nickels made no reply and each boy busied himself with his own thoughts. Collins broke the silence, knocking on the windshield.

"Hiya," Collins said pleasantly. "Am I interrupting anything?"

"No, Mr. Collins," Nickels said quickly, relief showing in his face. "No! Wait. We're getting right out."

"Hear there was a little difficulty at practice," Collins said lightly.

No one spoke and Collins continued slowly, "Lots of talk going around town about it and I thought you might like to know." He wasn't speaking directly to Byrnes but it was clear to all of them that the pitcher was the target. "Most of the fellows I heard talking seemed to feel you might be making a mistake."

Collins waited for a reaction but none came. After a brief pause he continued, speaking in a gentle voice. "When a team's going bad, fellows, why that's when every player on the squad ought to dig in and put out for all he's worth."

One would have thought Collins was talking to himself as far as a response or a change of expression on the faces of his listeners was concerned. Not a boy moved. Collins went on. "I don't like to ask *anyone* for personal favors, but I'd sure appreciate it a lot if you'd all show up in uniform tomorrow." He cleared his throat and waited expectantly.

Nick Nickels made the break. Nick took a deep breath and then the words came fast and furious. "I guess you know how we feel about you, Mr. Collins. We'd do anything for you. All of us! So far, me and Lefty are the only ones who turned in our uniforms. Murph and Belter and Bob aren't in it at all!"

Byrnes swung out of the taxi and walked around to the sidewalk. "Neither are you," he said sharply. "The whole deal is mine and I can take care of myself." He turned to Collins. "I feel the same way as Nick, Mr. Collins, but I can't *beg* to get back on the squad."

"Beg to get back," Collins echoed. "Why, Lefty, Rockwell didn't cut you. Why, I understand you made the decision yourself. Simply walked out! That right?"

Byrnes shook his head indecisively. "Well, maybe, I guess," he hedged.

"Well, then," Collins said brightly, "all you have to do is show up tomorrow and that's all there is to it. Right?"

Byrnes shook his head. "It's not that easy, Mr. Collins."

"But why? Listen, I've got an idea. S'pose I go see the coach myself. S'pose I tell him you made a mistake and that you'll be out there tomorrow swinging for all you're worth. O.K.?"

Again Byrnes shook his head. "No, Mr. Collins, I prefer to work it out myself. Thanks, though."

Nickels made the better suggestion. "It's our place to go to the coach, Mr. Collins. I don't know about Lefty, but I think I'll be out there tomorrow."

"Me too!" Gillen added.

"We'll work it out," Nickels said softly. "Thanks a lot for your help. You're— Well, you're swell and we all appreciate your friendship."

Jim Collins drove out to the farm that night with a light heart. Next to the members of a fellow's own family there is nothing quite so wonderful as giving a helping hand to a bewildered youngster. Most kids need someone to lean on when they make the first break away from home, and it is in this vital period of their lives that lifelong impressions are made. Collins was the kind of man who made the right impression on a kid, and although he was never to know, he was the direct reason for the decision which the five youngsters made shortly after his departure.

The rift in the ranks of the Fence Busters had been common knowledge to all the fans. To the sports re-reporters, too. Not the least interested spectator at that Thursday's practice had been Gil Mack, publicity director for the university and sports editor of the *Statesman*, State's weekly school paper. Mack had followed the fortunes of the Fence Busters ever since the day he had watched the first practice session and had given the team its name. And Mack had been greatly disillusioned when his Fence Busters fell off in their hitting and began to lose games.

The sports writer had been more than a little disgusted when the youngsters began concentrating on the fences and their batting averages instead of team play. Mack was on Rockwell's side all the way. He had appreciated the problem and had marveled at the patience of the veteran coach. Trying to help, Gil had previously written several sharp columns about the selfishness of the stars, and the scene which he had observed and sized up on Thursday afternoon gave him another chance to pour it on Byrnes and his companions. Mack really went to town the next morning in the *Statesman*.

# FENCE BUSTERS RIFT COMES TO A SHOWDOWN

## Lefty Byrnes and Nick Nickels Turn in Their Uniforms

### By GIL MACK

Coach Henry Rockwell has coached hundreds of youngsters in the thirty-odd years he has been interested in baseball and he has undoubtedly met a lot of temperamental ball-players. However, he must feel that the present crop of would-be stars whom this writer erroneously tagged the Fence Busters must top them all. Questioned last evening following the resignation of two disgruntled players, Coach Rockwell stated that there wasn't room on the freshman squad for any athlete who wouldn't hustle.

This writer agrees and feels that there are at least three more frosh regulars who ought to start hustling. This conclusion is based on firsthand observation of recent practices. The desultory performance of several regulars is a clear indication

that they not only feel it unnecessary to hustle but believe they can practice when and how they please. Byrnes and Nickels will be missed, but there are other capable hurlers. Soapy Smith, for instance, is a first-class receiver. The regulars referred to above are Bob Emery, Murph Gillen, and Belter Burke. This reporter has felt for some time that the outfield trio was resting on their early-season laurels and should be benched.

Going further, it might be wise to give Speed Morris a jolt. The clever little shortstop seems to have lost much of the aggressive play which made him a standout in the pre-season drills.

This column's hat is off to Coach Rockwell and his avowed determination to limit freshman uniforms to players who want to play hustling baseball . . .

The story wasn't as critical as it might have been, but it brought a lot of repercussions. Henry Rockwell didn't like it and called Gil Mack to express his displeasure.

Rock felt that Mack had interpreted his statement about hustling in a manner which was derogatory to the players and he was extremely upset. He wasn't the only one who was upset. Lefty Byrnes, Nick Nickels, Bob Emery, Murph Gillen, and Belter Burke were completely demoralized.

The quintet had threshed out their baseball problem after Jim Collins' departure the previous evening and out of the meeting had come a resolve to forget the past. Lefty Byrnes had gone along with Nickels and had agreed to see Rockwell and ask for another chance. They met for lunch at their usual eating place but they weren't in the mood for food. Byrnes was bitterly sarcastic.

"Ask Rockwell for another chance, huh? Swell! Just swell! I wouldn't ask him for the time of day! I'm glad, now, we didn't let Jim Collins talk to Rockwell. Then we *would* feel like two cents! Temperamental! Won't be missed! Hustling baseball! Huh!"

"No room," Burke snorted. "Would-be stars!"

Nick Nickels took a different view. The big catcher felt that there was some mistake. "I don't believe the coach said that," he mused. "He's not that kind of man. Mack's clever. He can twist words around so that black spells white."

Bob Emery couldn't see where it mattered. "So what?" he asked.

"So we don't play any more baseball," Burke said shortly.

"I do," Gillen remonstrated. "At least I go out and try! Any of you guys going with me?"

"Let's think about it," Nickels said slowly. "I think we ought to stick together one way or the other."

"There's only one way for me," Gillen said firmly. "I want to play ball."

Gillen meant what he said, for he was the only member of the group who made an appearance that afternoon. Surprisingly, their absence drew little or no comment. Rockwell had expected that it would turn out that way and Red Schwartz, Fireball Finley, Soapy Smith, and sundry members of the pitching staff were far from displeased. And, just like that, something happened to the morale of the ball club. It was evident in the hustle and in the chatter and in the catcalls and in the good-natured insults which flew from player to player.

The hustle and spirit carried over to Saturday morning and resulted in a smashing 7–1 victory over Midwestern Prep. Fireball Finley led the assault with the willow, getting three for four and playing brilliantly in the field. Schwartz hit but one for four, but he covered left field like a blanket. Soapy walked twice, flied out to left, and laced a two-bagger to center in four trips to the plate. Chip played the entire game, getting one for two and walking three times. Henry Rockwell breathed a big sigh of relief and pleasure when it was over. This was his kind of ball club.

So far as the Valley Falls contingent was concerned, it was quite a day. They had something to write home about. The game marked the first time all five members had played in the same game.

Speed Morris? It didn't look as if he was going to make it but he did. In the bottom of the eighth, Rockwell made it one-hundred-percent representation when he sent Speed in to pinch-hit for Eddie Anderson.

That Sunday was a memorable one at the Collins farm. It was Cindy's eighteenth birthday and Fireball was master of ceremonies. He had picked the guests. There were six or eight of them, most of them selected from his Valley Falls friends—Soapy, Biggie Cohen,

Speed Morris, Red Schwartz—all of them except Chip Hilton. He had been the first to be invited, to be sure. However, someone had to keep the home fires burning at State Drug. Even though the afternoon turned cold and rainy and business was quiet, Chip persuaded Soapy and Fireball that he could take care of the fountain for them and bone up on some irregular verbs at the same time.

Fireball had appealed to Mitzi for help, and she had offered to get her younger sister to come over and look after the fountain during the afternoon and evening, but Chip could not be persuaded, even by Cindy's father when he came to town to pick up the boys. Chip saw them off with a smile and a box of George Grayson's best chocolates for the birthday girl. He noticed that Eddie Anderson and one or two other boys on the freshman baseball team were crowded in the Collins car.

Chip really did not know why he had refused the invitation to attend the party at the Collins farm. He really loved a farm, especially one like the Collins' with its big barns, rolling acres and comfortable farmhouse, and open hospitality. Mitzi looked at him thoughtfully when he turned back into the store after seeing Jim Collins and his friends drive away.

The boys, led by Soapy, sang State songs on the way out, and made up in volume what they lacked in harmony. Cindy met them at the doorway that led to the great room which served as kitchen and dining room. She was wearing a bright yellow blouse which seemed to bring cheer to even so dull a day. It was the color of spring daffodils, and her lovely young face wore a smile of greeting to match it.

Biggie Cohen and one or two others went out to the

barns with Jim Collins to help with the chores, while
the rest of the boys put themselves at the disposal of
the young hostess. Soon they were busily, if not too
helpfully, employed. And somehow, among the noisy
confusion and the horseplay, the table got set. Jim
Collins and his aides came stomping in from the chores,
and a few moments later they were all sitting down at
the bountifully supplied birthday table.

Soapy stared restlessly at the heaped-up platters
while Cynthia opened her gifts with happy squeals of
delight. At last Jim Collins said a short grace and then
they all fell to work on the delicious food which Cindy
had spent all that day and the day before in preparing.
It was a happy occasion and the rafters of that great
room rang with shouts of laughter and bursts of song.
They missed Chip Hilton, but his absence could not
possibly have dampened that carefree evening of fun
and celebration.

Then Fireball brought in the cake he had ordered
sent out from town. It was lighted by eighteen candles,
and Cindy's eager, excited, sweet face hovered above
the soft glow of the candlelight, ready to blow them
out. One of the boys ran into the sitting room and began to pound out "Happy Birthday" on the piano.
Everybody stood up and the strains of that festive song
rang out above Cindy's happy laughter.

And then it happened! Some thought it was a spark
from one of the candles which the girl had blown out.
Some blamed the doughnut which had hurtled across
the table and struck one of the candles. In an instant Cindy's beautiful blouse was ablaze. While she
screamed in fright and anguish, Fireball whipped off
his jacket and threw it around her, smothering the
flames. Jim Collins almost tipped over the table in his

hurry to get to his daughter's side. Waving the boys back, he seized the girl in his arms and rushed into the sitting room. The group of boys seemed paralyzed over the sudden disaster. No one spoke. No one moved. Only Fireball seemed to have his wits about him. The telephone hung on the wall near the door. With one bound he reached it and began to call the General Hospital at University. Not until he was assured that the ambulance was on the way, and a surgeon accompanying it, did he turn to face the room. His awed schoolmates saw that he was crying. A few moments later they heard the bell of a speeding ambulance. In another moment it was at the door.

It was late when the boys got back to town. Jim Collins and Fireball had accompanied the ambulance to the hospital. They turned out the lights in that now silent room, which only a short time before had been the scene of so much merrymaking.

Only a few words were spoken on that dark, rainy night as the members of the frosh baseball team made their way back to town.

"Gosh, I hope she—"

"Second-degree burn—that's awful!"

"How'll we ever face it if—?"

"Let's not tell Chip—"

"He's bound to find out—"

"I wish I didn't ever have to go back to school—"

It was late when Chip locked up the drugstore that Sunday night. He had been expecting Soapy and Fireball to stop in on the way home to report on the good time they had had at the birthday party. When they had not come by eleven, he turned out the lights and locked up the empty store. He was even more astonished not to find Soapy in their room when he reached the dormitory. And when Chip woke up on Monday morning he found his usually irrepressible roommate strangely subdued in spirits. It might have been better if Soapy had confided in Chip what was on his mind that blue-Monday morning. The double disaster that hung over the Collins home had left the redhead in a tail spin which he did not seem to want Chip to share.

While the old fight and hustle was still there when the frosh team took the field against Ramsey Seminary that afternoon, nothing seemed to happen. Finley couldn't hit the size of his hat and Soapy was worse. Morris and Schwartz tried too hard, and the ever-dependable Biggie could do nothing right.

Chip was murderous with the stick and faultless in the field but his performance wasn't enough and they dropped the game by a 6–5 score and hit the bottom of the well in spirits. The Seminary chucker didn't have a thing and Chip couldn't figure it out. Rockwell added to the confusion by sending Murph Gillen up to hit for Cohen in the ninth. It was the first time in Chip's memory that Rockwell had used a pinch hitter for the hard-hitting first baseman. But it turned out to be a bad move. At least so far as results were concerned. Gillen hit the two-and-one pitch right back to the hurler for the third out.

Low in spirits and baffled by the sudden collapse of his teammates, Chip couldn't figure it out. What had happened?

Soapy knew the answer. The redhead found it difficult to keep a secret at any time but it was almost impossible for him to refrain from telling Chip. Talking to a morose Fireball that evening at work he broached the thought.

"I oughta tell Chip, Fireball."

"Nothing doing!"

"But why? Heck, Speed and Biggie and Red know about it. Why not Chip?"

But Finley was adamant. "No! Chip's got enough trouble!"

# CHAPTER 16

## DOUBLE TROUBLE

JIM COLLINS missed the Monday heartbreaker. It was the first time State's Number One fan had missed a game in five years. Sick? Well, yes and no. Collins was all right physically but that was about as far as one could go. He had talked with the chief surgeon that morning. Cindy was out of danger. There would be no need for skin grafts and all that sort of thing. She was receiving the best of care, and in two weeks, perhaps, she would be home again. But the memory of that sudden flash and Cindy's agonizing scream still left him feeling sick. Nothing like this had happened in his life since that long-ago time when Cindy's mother had taken ill and died—all within one tragic week.

The excitement and grief of that Sunday night had almost driven from Jim's mind the slow endless worry of what was happening to the farm. Absently he picked up the Tuesday morning paper and turned to the sports page to see what his boys had been doing. The bold print at the top of the column told the story.

### FENCE BUSTERS LOSE AGAIN

#### Ramsey Seminary Surprises Frosh Stars 6–5

"Oh, no!" Collins muttered. "Not again!" He scanned the box score, noting the absence of Byrnes, Nickels,

157

Emery, and Burke from the line-up. "Now, what?" he said aloud. "Guess Rockwell's going to let them sit it out a little while. Anyway, Gillen got a chance."

Collins sat in the kitchen rocker a long time that morning. The chair had been his father's favorite for many years and it brought back poignant memories. Especially this morning. Later, when he started for town, his heart was filled with sadness. After a short call at the hospital he delayed the disagreeable task ahead of him as long as possible and exhausted every subterfuge before entering the bank. He spent a disagreeable fifteen minutes there, and as he came down the broad steps, ran smack into Fireball Finley. The big man's attitude toward Fireball had changed immensely since the athlete had proved to be a baseball player and especially after the events of Sunday night. But he had to force the smile of greeting.

"Hello, Fred. Too bad about the game. Can't win them all, though."

"We should have won that one. We couldn't do anything right. At least I couldn't. I couldn't seem to get Cynthia—"

Collins nodded his head understandingly. "Lots of people have days like that, Fireball," he said softly.

"Yes, but I was awful. I just seemed sort of numb."

"Guess you weren't the only one, Fred. Saw by the paper that Rockwell used Gillen. Probably didn't have a chance to use any of the others."

"They didn't show up for practice. I think they've quit for good."

"I don't understand that," Collins said slowly. "Why, they told me they were going to let bygones be bygones. Guess I'll pay Rockwell a little visit. See you later, Fred."

Collins was up to his neck in trouble, but his interest in State's fabulous freshmen overshadowed everything. He headed straight for the nearest telephone and made a date with Rockwell for lunch. When they met at the restaurant, Collins jumped right into the subject nearest his heart.

"Tough luck yesterday, Rock. Say, what happened to the Byrnes crowd?"

Rockwell smiled wryly. "Too many headlines, maybe, Jim. Some kids just can't take publicity."

"I don't believe that's it, Rock. You know, I talked to those kids last Thursday night—right after they walked off the field—and honest, Rock, they were all set to report back on Friday."

"That right? Wonder what happened?"

"You think Gil Mack's story might have—"

"I don't know whether it kept them from reporting," Rockwell interrupted, "but I do know it was uncalled for— I talked to Mack about it."

"You mind if I see those kids again?"

"Of course not. You know, Jim, I've worked with kids all my life and I've had only a handful who didn't come around—one way or another. I hate to see a kid sour-up like this Byrnes boy. He's all right deep down inside— most kids are—but I can't seem to get through that thick skin of his. I hope you can. He's worth saving."

Collins agreed with the coach, all right. But he was chiefly concerned about the great team he had rooted so strongly for early in the season. He reasoned that it was a shame to let a great team fall apart, just because a kid had the wrong slant on things.

That evening, after his chores were finished, Jim Collins drove to town to visit his daughter at the General Hospital. She kissed her dad as he stooped over her

bed. Never had she seen her father look so troubled—
or so old.

"What's wrong, Daddy?" she asked softly. "You aren't
worried about me, are you, silly? The doctor says I
might drown, but I couldn't really burn."

Jim shook his head and smiled gently.

"Why, those freshman baseballers of mine have got
me worried."

"Now, Daddy, you aren't being honest with me."

"I met Fireball this morning outside the bank. Finley didn't look very happy," Jim said.

"It isn't baseball that's worrying Fred. And I don't
think it's me," Cindy said. "I think he may be worrying
over the same thing that you are, Daddy. Please tell
me, dear."

And when Jim Collins left the General Hospital that
night he felt better than he had in months. He had told
his daughter of the trouble that had been hanging over
the farm for long, long months. And all the way out to
the lonely farmhouse he could hear Cindy's words:
"Don't you worry, dear. Nothing but good is going to
happen to us now!"

Later, while Fireball and Cindy were talking on the
telephone, Jim Collins was meeting with Lefty Byrnes
and his crowd at the taxi stand at State and Main. And
Jim was having just about as much luck with them as
he had had at the bank. The only member of the group
he could shake was Nick Nickels. The big catcher listened carefully and made his decision.

"I think you're right, Mr. Collins," Nick said soberly.
"I've acted like a spoiled brat. I'll be out there tomorrow."

Nick was as good as his word. He reported Wednesday afternoon prepared to take his lumps. Rockwell

never blinked an eyelash, merely nodded, and let it go at that. Perhaps that is the best way to handle such situations, anyway.

Nick Nickels couldn't be blamed for the occurrences that afternoon, of course, but someone put the jinx on the Fence Busters. Flash Sparks broke a small ankle bone in the sliding pit and Diz Dean complained of a sore arm.

Grant State came in for the Friday afternoon game and the jinx persisted. Chip played like a big-leaguer, but Fireball, Soapy, Biggie, and his other pals performed like junior high school scrubs. Rockwell used Nickels as a pinch hitter for Soapy in the seventh, but the layoff had hurt the big receiver and he struck out both times he came to bat. Grant walked home with the game by a score of 9 to 3.

Chip knew there was something seriously wrong with his friends. Biggie might have an off day with the stick, but he'd never falter in his fielding and throwing. "No," Chip mused, "there's something bothering the whole bunch. They just couldn't all go bad at the same time. Soapy knows too! Well, he'll tell me tonight or else!"

It wasn't easy. Soapy tried his best to cover up, but Chip gave him no rest. "Come on, Soapy," Chip urged. "I've got to know. There's too much at stake!"

"But, Chip, it—it doesn't concern you."

"Anything which upsets you and Biggie and Speed and Red concerns me. That goes for Fireball, too!"

"Well, if you've gotta know it's got something to do with Jim Collins!"

"Collins? You mean—"

"That's right! You know how all the guys feel about Mr. Collins. Well, he's got money trouble."

"What's that got to do with playing baseball?"

"Plenty! Fireball's all upset and he's got the rest of the guys in the same frame of mind. I'm worried too! I like Jim Collins as much as any man I ever knew."

Chip was puzzled. It didn't make sense. "For Pete's sake, Soapy," he said impatiently, "stop beating about the bush and tell me what it's all about."

Soapy took a deep breath and plunged. "Well, he's gonna lose the farm!"

"No! How?"

"Mortgage. The bank's gonna foreclose if he doesn't pay up his back interest installments."

"What's that got to do with playing ball?"

"But, Chip, don't you see? The bank—or, at least, the new president of the bank—says Collins pays more attention to baseball than he does to his farm—and, well, Fireball and Biggie and the rest of us feel like we ought to do something about it."

"Why?"

"Because he's been so nice to us, I guess. And because—because of Cynthia."

That was too much for Chip. He couldn't figure it out. Sure, he liked Mr. Collins a lot. And he could appreciate how the gang felt about the farm. But what did all that have to do with freshman baseball? And what about Cynthia?

Soapy started to talk. He told his roommate about the events of that tragic night at the Collins farm when the birthday party had come to such an unhappy end. He told how Cynthia had been taken to the hospital with second-degree burns, and how each of the boys who had been at the Collins' home that evening was feeling personally responsible for what had happened to Cynthia. How the shock of it all had affected their play.

"But, Soapy," cried Chip, "the Collinses are my friends also. I'm concerned about their trouble too! Here we've been buddies for years, and you leave me out. I don't get it!"

Soapy was demoralized. "But, Chip, I woulda told you first of all, but Fireball and Biggie said you'd had enough trouble—and, well, you sure have. Gee, Chip, you know I tell you everything."

"Forget it, Soapy. Tell me the rest of it."

Soapy brightened. "Well, Chip, it seems that the old president of the bank played ball with Mr. Collins in the old days and he never worried much about the farm payments. Then he died and the new president started throwin' his weight around and cracked down on past-due interest payments. It seems Mr. Collins is way behind and he can't raise the money. Fireball said he met him outside the bank yesterday morning and he was as white as a sheet. And this afternoon, just before the game, Cynthia told Fireball that the bank was goin' to foreclose in ten days. Gee, Chip, you think we could do something?"

Chip shrugged. "I don't know what, Soapy. Gosh, we haven't got any money. Only person I know with money is— Hey!"

Soapy's face lit up like a light. "You got an idea, Chip?"

"Maybe. Let me think about it."

Chip thought about it all evening and that night, too. He liked Jim Collins and he liked Cindy. But he found it difficult to reconcile his liking for them with the necessity of burdening his boss with a problem which was little or none of his concern. "Gosh," he mused aloud, "that would be an imposition and no fooling."

Imposition or not, Chip made up his mind to talk to

George Grayson. Jim Collins had been his friend and the friend of everyone else it seemed. Chip guessed there must be a good reason behind the old saw that to have a friend you have to be a friend.

But his resolution faltered when he reported for work the next morning. George Grayson passed the storeroom and poked his head through the doorway with a cheery good morning and Chip didn't make a move. But when Fireball checked in a little later with a long face and the manner of a whipped dog, Chip headed for the cashier's desk.

"You s'pose Mr. Grayson would spare me a few minutes, Mitzi?"

"He's pretty busy, Chip. But for you—of course! Go on up!"

Chip was not afraid of anyone but he would have preferred to tackle a battleship than walk up the steps to George Grayson's office that morning. But, as usual, his boss was friendly. George Grayson probably realized that a man made most headway in business when his employees were happy in their work. He greeted Chip warmly.

"What's on your mind, Chip?"

"Something I just have to talk to someone about, Mr. Grayson."

"Shoot, Chip. What is it? The team?"

"Well, I guess it's a combination of the team and Mr. Collins. You see the team hasn't been going very well and I think a lot of it is because Mr. Collins—"

Grayson took off his glasses, concern written on his face. "Jim? Can't understand that—"

"I don't mean it's his fault. It—it just concerns him."

"I've known Jim Collins a long time, Chip. We were classmates in high school. He was a fine ballplayer and he's been a fine influence for the kids in this town. I think a lot of Jim, Chip. Now what about him?"

That made it easy. For some reason, youngsters never seem to get it through their heads that they're surrounded by men and women who want to help them with their problems. No matter where a fellow lives, he can find any number of successful men and women who are ready and willing to help him. Grayson's receptive manner and friendly attitude were all Chip needed. He spilled the story easily and without hesitations. Grayson listened attentively until Chip finished.

"Jim Collins is a good man, Chip," Grayson said reflectively. He smiled. "No pun, now, but he deserves a lot of credit for what he's done for the kids. I guess he's done as much for the athletes at State as the Athletic Department. He's proud, too, Chip. Jim wouldn't ask anyone for help." His eyes twinkled and a friendly smile played across his lips. "Now, Chipper, what was the real reason you came to see me about Jim Collins? Cynthia Collins?"

Chip was embarrassed. "Golly, no, Mr. Grayson— why, I hardly know her. Honest! Why, she's Fireball's girl. And she's in the hospital!"

Grayson knew exactly how Chip felt about girls and he enjoyed Chip's confusion. If Mitzi Savrill couldn't charm this youngster, no one could. And he knew more about the Collins matter than Chip would ever know. But he said nothing more. He simply sent Chip away with the assurance that he would try to do something, but made no promises.

"You know, Chip," he said in his kindly voice, "it's a bit irregular for a board member to step in on bank policy—I think you understand. Now, I hope you'll say nothing about this conversation to anyone. All right?"

It was all right, but it didn't go far enough. During lunch hour he went over to the hospital to see Cindy. Chip felt that he had done all he could and he wished it would help the team. Especially that afternoon in the Midland game. Finley was no ball of fire, and Biggie and Soapy should have spent the afternoon in the library. Chip played brilliantly. He was errorless in the field and perfect at bat, getting four for four. And he hustled and drove his teammates for all he was worth. But it wasn't enough. Midland romped away with an easy 9–3 victory, and the chances of State being represented in the Little Four championship grew dimmer and dimmer.

Chip's heart was heavy but he got a lift out of the knowledge that George Grayson knew about the problem. Anyway, it gave him something to hope for; good news might come after the Monday board meeting at the bank; might be all that was needed to clear the air once and for all and get the Fence Busters back on their game. When he read the paper the next morning he knew for sure that the news had better be good. . . .

## MIDLAND ROMPS OVER FROSH

### Easy 9–3 Victory for Visitors

### Fence Busters Need Pitchers

### Coach Henry Rockwell Plans Shake-up

#### By BILL BELL

The fences at Alumni Field suffered little yesterday afternoon when Midland scored an easy victory over Henry Rockwell's fro-zen freshman baseball team. It was a fast, easy game for the Junior College outfit who surprised all concerned with a slim 130-pound pitcher who broke all the bats of the locals with the exception of Chip Hilton's. Silent Joe Maxim, Rockwell's only remaining chucker, was tired. Maxim has now worked two games in three days. Chip Hilton had a perfect day in the field and at bat, but the only other local who could register safely was Hutch Kroll. Hutch walked twice and hit twice and that was it —6 hits and 3 runs—all unearned.

After the dull performance, Coach Rockwell stated that there would be another shake-up in an effort to get the faltering Fence Busters back in the winning habit and that he would experiment with several youngsters in the hopes of finding someone who could help the pitching problem. The famed freshmen started out in grand fashion and this writer would like to see the same group of kids he tabbed the Fence Busters back in action again. That gang could hit as well as any ball club that ever dashed out on a State diamond. With the Little Four championship series only a few weeks away and with the Fence Busters slipping badly, something should be done to restore the original line-up.

Lefty Byrnes, Belter Burke, and Bob Emery liked the write-up. Strangely enough, they liked Bill Bell. For the first time, the trio agreed that the writer knew his baseball. "They need us," Byrnes gloated. "It takes a smart sports writer like Bell to figure out what's wrong. Wonder what Rockwell will think now. About time someone told him the score. He'd never figure it out himself!"

## CHAPTER 17

## COMEBACK KIDS

GEORGE GRAYSON was one of University's leading citizens. He took a prominent part in civic affairs but somehow managed to remain in the background. He was like that at the bank. One of the strongest men on the board, he usually went along with the majority and seldom interjected himself into an argument. Thomas Hemming, the former president of the bank, had given Grayson his start; he had guided him through his early days as a businessman and had been proud of his protégé's progress. After the death of Hemming, the members of the board had selected Charlie Stimley, the cashier, as the new president.

Stimley had long aspired to the position and had started right out to prove that the methods formerly employed were outmoded. He came bustling into the meeting with a sheaf of papers in his hand and called the meeting to order with a formality which seemed strangely out of place after the easygoing manner of his predecessor.

"Gentlemen," Stimley began briskly, "we have a full agenda this morning, so I would like to get right down to business. I have spent the past week checking through some of our long-past-due, perhaps I should say latent, mortgages, and I am shocked at the state of the accounts. I should like to have the authorization of the board to straighten them out and to foreclose where it is deemed necessary. Will someone put this authorization in the form of a motion?"

"I so move," Jud King said shortly.

"May I have a second to the motion?"

"Excuse me, gentlemen," Grayson interrupted. "Isn't it the purpose of these meetings to discuss particular mortgages and loans? I would like to know, for example, which mortgages are to be foreclosed."

To say that a shocked silence followed would be putting it mildly. None of those present had ever heard George Grayson express himself so strongly and the interruption completely upset Charlie Stimley.

Jud King was the first to recover. "Seems logical to me," he said. "I withdraw the motion."

"Well, that's all right," Stimley said nervously. "But there's a lot of them and there's quite a bit of business on the agenda."

"I'm not too busy to spare the time," Grayson said.

Grayson got support from the other members of the board on that point, and Stimley began to discuss the individual cases. Collins' account was the second on the list. It was most apparent from the tone of his voice that Charlie Stimley had fully made up his mind with respect to the Collins mortgage.

"The Collins note shows a balance of ten thousand dollars with unpaid installments of some four thousand dollars and accumulated interest amounting to twenty-four hundred dollars. I've talked to Collins and he says he is unable to meet the past-due payments and will find it difficult to meet the present year's interest. I gave him until today to raise the past-due amounts or face foreclosure proceedings."

"What about the potential of the farm?" Grayson asked.

"What do you mean?"

"I mean, is the farm capable of supporting the mortgage? Or of supporting an increase?"

"Increase?" Stimley echoed. "Why, with that baseball-crazy man in charge of the farm, the mortgage isn't worth the paper it's written on. He hasn't made a payment in years. Made no effort to make a payment."

"I know the farm well," Grayson said evenly, eying his fellow board members. "It's a good farm and Jim is a good farmer. He's had a few setbacks but he's all right. Why, the farm timber alone is worth ten or fifteen thousand dollars. He's got some wonderful maple trees that are going to be worth a lot of money some day. I'm in favor of incorporating the unpaid interest into a new note and extending the mortgage."

"How in the world can you justify such procedure?" Stimley demanded.

"Partly on the value of the farm," Grayson said softly, "but chiefly on the value of the man."

"Value of the man?" Stimley said incredulously. "That—that foul ball?"

"That's right, Mr. Stimley. That foul ball, as you call him, has done more to set the kids of this town right than anyone I know. Men like Jim Collins are priceless to any community. I'm quite sure there's nothing wrong with his finances that a little time will not straighten out. I suggest we issue a new mortgage."

Jud King, Bill Hopkins, Sam Snyder, and T. C. Train couldn't figure this thing out. George Grayson always went along with the president or a consensus. There was something going on here they didn't understand. What was it all about?

Stimley made a mistake, then, by interpreting their silence as disapproval. He decided to take a definite stand. "There will be no new mortgage, Mr. Grayson," he said firmly. "As the president of this bank, I cannot jeopardize the money entrusted to my care."

"I see," Grayson said gently. He rose slowly to his feet, smiling slightly as he spoke, "Under the circumstances, I believe the only course left to me is to resign as a director of this bank."

In the stunned silence which followed, Grayson turned to face his fellow directors. "It has always been my belief that this bank stood as an organization dedicated to the service of the community in good times and bad. An organization ready and anxious to serve its citizens—not as a profit-making institution measuring its progress by the exploitation of properties it might be able to seize through the misfortunes of the residents of the community, but—"

Sam Snyder leaped to his feet. "George," he remonstrated, "this is ridiculous."

"That's right," Hopkins reiterated. "Downright silly. Of course we're the friends of the citizens of the community. You—"

"Excuse me, gentlemen," Train interrupted. "May I inject a word? Wait, George—

"Gentlemen, Tom Hemming and I founded this bank forty-three years ago. Tom dedicated his life to this bank and this community. I guess I know what he stood for better than any other living man—and, gentlemen, George Grayson is right! Tom Hemming always stood by his customers in times of need. He built this bank on the cornerstone of friendship. It shall not change!"

Only the persons in that room knew what transpired after that declaration. Suffice it to say that George Grayson reconsidered his resignation and Jim Collins got the surprise of his life half an hour later when he walked into the office of the bank's president and was received with smiling graciousness.

For one heart-rending second Collins believed that Charlie Stimley was being nice only because it was necessary to transmit bad news. But Stimley's words belied the impression.

"Glad to see you, Jim," Stimley said, rising from his desk and extending his hand. "I've got good news for you. The bank has decided to issue a new mortgage incorporating the back interest in a new note and making the payments a little easier."

"What! Oh, boy! What a relief! Thanks, Mr. Stimley, thanks a million."

"Don't thank me, Jim. Confidentially, you might buy George Grayson a cigar the next time you see him, but keep me out of it."

"You don't say! Hmmmmmm. Don't get it!"

"Is it necessary?"

Collins was thinking that it was, but he decided that it could wait. Right now, he wanted to see Cindy and he headed in the right direction—straight for the General Hospital. Later, he'd call at State Drug to see George Grayson.

Cynthia Ann was waiting for her father with an anxious heart. She tried to cover up, to be carefree and vivacious, but she wasn't fooling Fireball who was sitting in a chair by the window. Finley tried to play the game, too. But he wasn't too successful.

"Well, kids, guess what?" shouted Jim as he entered

the room. He chuckled when he saw the anxious look in Cindy's eyes.

A moment later he was telling them the wonderful news. Never were there two happier youngsters in a hospital room.

"Didn't I tell you, Daddy, that we were out of the woods?" Cindy cried.

"It's our woods that the bank's giving me a new mortgage on!" Jim shouted. "From this day on, I'm working like a holy Trojan to make that farm of ours pay," Jim Collins promised solemnly.

Chip Hilton was in the storeroom at State Drug. Good news travels fast, and it already had reached him in the storeroom at State Drug. Maybe the Fence Busters would wake up now. Now that there wouldn't be any more girl trouble and sympathy trouble to jinx the bats. He felt the elbow of his right arm. Felt good. Doc Terring said he could start throwing righty any time now. He wasn't ready for any heavy-duty pitching assignments but it wouldn't be long now. Maybe he ought to try a few windups. . . .

And that's what he was doing when Jim Collins cautiously opened the door and said hello. "Hiya, Chip. Loosening up the old wing? How soon's that old soupbone going to be ready? Can't be very long, now, I hope."

"Feels good, Mr. Collins. Doc Terring said I could start pitching again in about a week."

"That's great, Chip. Say—" Collins' face sobered. "Chip, I want to thank you for— Well, for what you did. It gave me a new lease on life. Honest."

"Wait a minute, Mr. Collins. I don't know what you're talking about. You're all mixed up."

"That's what George told me you'd say, Chip. Let's

leave it that way. One thing is sure, Chip. I'm not mixed up now. I guess I was until—well, until today. Anyway, I guess words can't speak for a man's heart. Good luck, Champ."

Chip thought it over. Collins knew he had talked to Mr. Grayson all right. So what? He hadn't done anything.

Collins didn't stop with Chip. He had to tell his other kids and headed straight for Wilson Dormitory. They weren't there, but he soon located Byrnes, Burke, and Emery at a corner table in the campus snack bar. It didn't take him long to tell the good news.

"This calls for a celebration," Byrnes exulted.

"We could make it a real big celebration and make everyone happy if you fellows would report for baseball tomorrow," Collins countered. "Why not? Guess you saw what Bill Bell wrote. Why, Rockwell would be tickled pink to have you back."

"What makes you say that?"

"Because I asked him. Look, kids. Everyone in town knows you three fellows are the difference between a spot in the Little Four series and just another season. C'mon, what do you say?"

"I'll never play for Rockwell," Byrnes said decisively. "Rockwell and Hilton dug the hole they're in—let them dig their way out of it."

"You've got Chip all wrong, Lefty," Collins said earnestly. "He's a good kid. Let me tell you something else. If it hadn't been for him, I'd never have gotten a break at the bank."

"Hilton! What did he have to do with it?"

"Everything! Honest!"

Byrnes snorted. "Huh! He tell you?"

Collins smiled resignedly. "I guess it's no use. No,

Lefty, Chip never said a word before nor after. In fact, he pretended he knew nothing about it."

"What makes you think he did?"

"Because the only man in University who could have gotten me the break told me flatly that he did it only because of Chip."

Byrnes shook his head disgustedly. "I don't get it," he said, shrugging his shoulders. "Where does *he* get all the drag?"

"I don't know where he gets it, Lefty. But it's my hunch that he works for it. Aw, come on, Lefty. Give it another try."

Byrnes shook his head stubbornly. "Nothing doing! Why, I wouldn't pitch for Rockwell if it meant the championship. And I know how much he'd like to win that! No, sir! Count me out! Period!"

"Well," Collins said wryly, "you three fellows are going to cost the team the championship. They just haven't got enough power without you. What's more important right now, Rockwell's only got two pitchers left—Maxim and Dean. And they're both dead tired."

"Why doesn't he use Nick and Murph?" Emery demanded.

"He is using them, but right now he needs pitching."

"Oh, sure," Byrnes said bitterly. "I'd go out there and he'd let me sit the bench just like Nick and Murph."

"No," Collins said defensively, "I don't think Rock would let anyone sit the bench if it meant a victory. I sure wish you'd change your mind."

"Nothing doing," Byrnes said shortly. "Not me!"

"Well," Collins said forlornly, "I guess there's nothing more I can do. Seems like I never can help—"

Jim Collins wasn't quite right about the last part of his unfinished observation. He had already performed his good deed. The news he had personally received that day was just what the doctor ordered as far as some of the key Fence Busters were concerned. And starting the following afternoon they began to prove that even the experts can be wrong about a ball club.

Strader Teachers caught the full onslaught the following afternoon. Biggie and Soapy and Fireball and Chip climbed all over three of the Teachers' chuckers, giving Silent Joe Maxim an easy 15–3 win. Maxim just reared back, kicked, and threw the ball. His support did the rest. And it worked!

That was only the start. They made Gil Mack and Bill Bell and Jim Collins forget Byrnes and his two hard-hitting pals by thumping the daylights out of North, giving Diz Dean an 11–0 whitewash victory. Dean followed Maxim's method and again it worked.

And they kept it up! They took to the road Friday and Saturday, Maxim beating Strader Friday afternoon, and Dean taking the first game of a double-header from North on Saturday morning. Rockwell pulled a big surprise by sending Soapy Smith to the hill in the afternoon and the redhead came through like a twenty-game winner. So, when they started back for University Saturday night, the Fence Busters were back in the running for a spot in the championship series.

University fans had watched the comeback of the frosh with real appreciation, but there were a few people in town who were not particularly enthused. Lefty Byrnes was one of these. Lefty was having a hard time figuring it out. Like a lot of others, Lefty was puzzled by the about-face of the Fence Busters. Lefty had a lot of time to think while driving his taxicab each night. Indeed, he did a lot of cogitating while on the job.

It was a busy Saturday night and Lefty got a call to pick up a Mr. Grayson in the college section of University. Two men were waiting to be driven to the airport. Although he was thinking about other matters, Lefty listened idly to the remarks of his two passengers as he drove toward the airport. But his ears pricked up when George Grayson mentioned the Fence Busters.

"Looks as if the freshman ball club is back in stride. Glad to see it."

"This Hilton boy works for you, doesn't he?"

"Been with me since last fall. Fine kid."

"Got a kick out of you setting Charlie Stimley down last Monday. Charlie's been moving a little too fast."

Grayson grunted. "Oh, I guess he's all right. Just trying to do a good job. By the way, John, I wouldn't even have known about Collins' predicament if Hilton hadn't brought it to my attention. He's a loyal kid, and he's done a lot of good things around this town. Modest, too. Won't take any credit."

"I've seen him around the store. Seems to keep busy."

"He's a hustler. A real ballplayer, too. Let me give you some idea of his way of thinking. I talked to him tonight when he got back on the job after the big win this afternoon at North. Well, he didn't even want to talk about the game. He was looking ahead to the Carleton series. He was talking about a pitcher by the name of Byrnes."

Lefty involuntarily glanced in the mirror. This was too much! Hilton again!

Grayson continued after a brief pause. "Chip said the team would breeze through if this pitcher would only play. Seems to have the idea it's his own fault that this other pitcher quit the team. Some sort of a kid misunderstanding, I guess. Too bad!"

"Seems as if there would be plenty of room for both of them," Grayson's companion observed. "Hard to understand why kids can't get that through their heads. Especially when they're both good."

# CHAPTER 18

## BEAN-BALL VICTORY

CHIP reared back, kicked, and poured a fast one straight into the center of the strike zone. Terring grimaced slightly as the speeding ball buried itself in the glove, but his face was wreathed in smiles when he called for the same pitch. "That's the ticket, Chip! Give me the same thing now. Same spot!"

Fifteen minutes later, Terring called it a day. "Nice throwing, kid. The old wing is coming around fast."

"How fast?" Chip queried.

"Well, I'd say fast enough, considering everything," Terring said slowly.

"You think I'll be ready by Saturday?" Chip persisted.

"Now, Chip, I just can't look at your arm and give you a green light. Just because you puff up the hand of an old codger like me."

179

"But I've been throwing hard for over a week now and my arm never felt better."

"Playing catch isn't the same as pitching a game, Chip."

"No, but I've been throwing curves and sliders and the fast one and, gosh, Doc, my arm feels swell. Why, I can put everything I've got into my knuckler and it doesn't hurt a bit. Look, Doc," Chip continued earnestly, "Rock hasn't got a single pitcher left and we've got to play Carleton two games, Friday and Saturday. Maybe a third on Monday if we split the first two."

Terring nodded grimly. "You're telling me! Or has it ever come to your attention that the coach happens to be my special pal. I guess he tells me more of his troubles than Mrs. Rockwell. I know the situation, all right."

"But if I'm right, Doc— If my arm is well, why can't I pitch?"

"Because we haven't worked enough for one thing. Further, you couldn't pitch both games even if you *were* right. I'd say you might be able to pitch one of the week-end games or part of a game, but right now I'm not sure. You come up here every day and we'll work a little each day all week and then we'll see. But I don't want you to say a word to the coach or anyone else. Understand? If Hank starts counting on you, and then it's no go, it will just about break his heart. Right?"

Chip nodded glumly and started back to Jeff. On the way, he was doing some real thinking. Maxim and Dean and Sparks were out for the season. Soapy could throw the ball over the plate but he was no pitcher. He wasn't equipped to cope with a tough team like Carleton.

"That leaves me," Chip murmured, "and I'm an uncertainty. Doc didn't seem too optimistic. I'm right, though, I know it!"

Just before he reached the dormitory, Chip got an idea. He stopped in his tracks and thought about it a few seconds. Then he made a decision, pivoted about, and headed in the other direction.

Right about then, Lefty Byrnes was reading Bill Bell's column. And there was a sour expression on his face as he read:

## STATE FROSH TAKE DOUBLE BILL AT NORTH
### Defeat North, 11–0; 14–10

Rockwell's Rail Splitters, rapidly supplanting Gil Mack's Fence Busters in local fan acclaim, came through with a surprising double win over North yesterday morning and afternoon to run their sudden and surprising victory skein to five games in a row.

In my book this is an almost unbelievable feat, carved out by a bunch of hustlers who had to depend upon two tired pitchers and a converted catcher for mound duty, as well as a makeshift line-up which included players with glass arms, injured arms, football knees, and paper ankles. All this leads this writer to quote a well-worn adage that it's an ill wind that doesn't blow some good.

Personally, I wish to extend my congratulations to Coach Henry Rockwell for a job well done. This, in the face of the crucial two- (possibly three-) game series with powerful Carleton who will be here next Friday and Saturday to play for the sole remaining spot in the Little Four championship.

So win or lose or draw, Rock, this corner's hat is off to you and your Rail Splitters. And as a friend of yours once said to me: "The Rock? Look, Bill Bell! He can take it!" And I think you can. Frankly, I wouldn't be surprised if you took Carleton and all the marbles in the Little Four series. Good luck, Coach. Keep 'em hustling.

Byrnes smashed the paper into a ball and threw it angrily into a corner. "Just luck," he muttered, "just plain fool's luck!"

He was still sitting there, thinking about the Fence Busters and his trouble with Rockwell and Chip, when someone called up from the hall downstairs to advise him that Chip Hilton was waiting and would like to see him.

Byrnes was surprised and puzzled. "Hilton!" he managed. "What does that guy want to see me about?" He walked slowly down the steps and braced himself for the meeting.

Chip came right to the point. "Hello, Lefty. Sorry to break in on you like this, but it's important." He hesitated a second and then hurried on. "Someone had to make the break, though—and, well, here I am."

"What's on your mind?" Byrnes asked abruptly.

"Well, Joe, Maxim and Diz Dean both have sore arms and we've got two games with Carleton next week end. If we could win them we'd be in the championship series."

"I know that!" Byrnes said shortly. "So what?"

"Just that we need you out there to win one of those games. Some of us were talking, and we figured that if you would come out and get loosened up, you could win the Friday game for us and we might be able to struggle through the Saturday game with Soapy or someone. Anyway, a win on Friday would guarantee us a split for the week end and you could go again next Monday if you had to— What do you say?"

Byrnes shrugged. "Why should I pitch for Rockwell?"

"It isn't for Rockwell," Chip said patiently, "it's for the team."

Byrnes had no answer for that one. He just sat there

mulling it over. But he wasn't thinking about the pitching or Rockwell. He was thinking about Chip Hilton. Lefty couldn't convince himself that his hated pitching rival would sacrifice his pride to ask for help. But he felt a glow of self-satisfaction. This was more like it. Chip Hilton had come to him. Well, it was about time someone woke up. Hitting was important, all right, but good pitching was the key to pennants in the big leagues and it was even more important in college ball.

Lefty was thinking that Chip Hilton was smarter than he'd figured. Smarter than Rockwell, anyway. But he couldn't bring himself to believe that Chip had only the success of the team in mind. "There's a catch in this somewhere," he told himself. "And I'm going to find out what it is!"

"How do I know Rockwell will let me suit up even if I do come out?" he demanded.

"Because he said he would," Chip said firmly. "Doc Terring has been working on my arm and he said Rockwell told him just today that your suit was still in your locker where you put it and he'd like to have you back. He said he thought we could go clear through if you came back. The gang would sure like to have you back too. I guess you know that."

Chip could sense that Byrnes was considering the idea, but there was no assurance of consent in Lefty's face. Then Chip got some unexpected assistance. Nick Nickels and Murph Gillen arrived on the scene. They were surprised to see Chip. But when they learned the reason for his presence, they quickly joined forces with him and added their support.

"What happened when you went out, Nick?" Byrnes demanded. "Rockwell bawl you out in front of the whole team?"

"Of course not," Nick said impatiently. "I told you

what happened. He didn't say a word. He acted like nothing had ever happened."

"That's right," Gillen agreed.

Byrnes eyed Chip doubtfully. "All right," he said reluctantly, "I'll be out tomorrow afternoon."

"You think you can get Emery and Burke to come out?" Chip asked.

Byrnes nodded. "Sure," he said. "They'll do anything I do. They'll be there."

The unruly pitcher went to bed that night feeling better than he had for a long time. But he was worried about the meeting with Rockwell. "I'll walk right off the field if he says anything," Byrnes told himself. "I'm not going to be pushed around by that guy any more."

The appearance of the unpredictable chucker with Bob Emery and Belter Burke the following afternoon created a mild sensation. Most of the players greeted them warmly. Chip was one of these, but his Valley Falls buddies were more reserved. They had no use for quitters! Period!

Byrnes tried all that week to figure out why he had reversed his stand and reported back for the team. He had been hurt and puzzled when Nick and Murph deserted him and had decided to go back and take their lumps. Lefty couldn't figure how anyone could swallow his pride and sit the bench and watch someone with half his ability playing regular. It didn't add up to Lefty.

"I'd never do it," Lefty muttered time and again. "Well, they came to me! Now, I'm going to show Nick and Murph and Hilton and Rockwell and everyone else what a *real* chucker can do. I guess the whole bunch knows now who they had to turn to for help, to pull the team out of the hole."

Lefty Byrnes was a strange youngster. A strange mixture of good and bad. He had turned down a big-league baseball offer so that he might strive for a college education. He had known the difficulties he would encounter. There had been no money available at home to help with his college expenses, but Lefty had decided to give it a try. He had landed the taxi job and the income from his driving and the benefits of a tuition scholarship were making it possible for him to achieve his ambition. Not that it was easy. Driving a taxicab six nights a week from seven o'clock to midnight kept a fellow hustling— hustling to get enough sleep and to keep up with the books and the classes. The addition of baseball meant that study was a *must* every minute of the day not spent in class.

Bill Bell and Gil Mack gave the Fence Busters plenty of space that week, and on Friday the stands were packed before five o'clock for the twilight game with Carleton. Chip was out on the field early, anxious to show Rockwell that his arm was right, hoping that Doc Terring would appear and give the good news to the coach. But Terring failed to show up and Chip reluctantly went out to right field to chase the hard-hit flies Jim Collins was delightedly lifting high in the air and clear to the fences.

Lefty Byrnes was warming up in front of the dugout, throwing to Nick Nickels, while Soapy Smith forlornly played catch with Eddie Anderson out in the bull pen. Joe Maxim and Diz Dean didn't even bother to limber up. Both were bitterly nursing their sore arms in the dugout.

But when the Fence Busters ran out for their fielding just before the start of the game, Soapy Smith was behind the plate. That was hard for Nick Nickels to take.

He figured to be the catcher with Lefty Byrnes pitching. But Henry Rockwell hadn't finished his reconstruction job with Nick Nickels. It still needed a little more time. So Nick sat in the dugout beside Bob Emery, Belter Burke, and Murph Gillen, and watched the Fence Busters out on the field. Henry Rockwell shot a quick glance in their direction when he went out to fungo to the infield, but none of the quartet saw him.

Rockwell's heart was light for the first time in weeks. Not because he had his Fence Busters intact again, but because he felt that Lefty Byrnes, Nick Nickels, Murph Gillen, Bob Emery, and Belter Burke were growing up and had begun to realize that baseball was a team game. A game where every player was entitled to a chance and that it was no disgrace to sit the bench. That is, if one could do it and cheer one's teammates in the field. "Well," he reflected, "the rest is up to them. They've made a good start. I'll just do a little watching now and see how they come out."

Chip was in right field. And when Rockwell lined them out for the throws to the plate, Chip blazed the ball back with his right arm straight as a string and with a perfect one-bounce hop.

Byrnes got away to a good start, striking out the lead-off hitter and getting the next two hitters on easy infield grounders. The fans weren't too friendly when Byrnes walked out to the hill to start the game, but they gave him a good hand coming back. And as the innings slipped away and Byrnes continued to throttle the Carleys, the applause grew in volume and enthusiasm each time he walked back to the dugout.

Carleton started a tall, slender southpaw on the mound. And he was fast, lightning fast. Furthermore, he was pitching tight, using the "brush back" on every power hitter who was trying to get a toehold at the plate. So State's Fence Busters, Fireball Finley, Biggie Cohen, and Chip couldn't dig in and couldn't lace into the ball. The game turned into a pitchers' duel.

It was a fast defensive game but far from dull. Each inning the goose eggs fell steadily in line on the scoreboard, and before the players and fans could believe it possible, it was the bottom of the ninth and neither team had scored.

Biggie Cohen led off and went down swinging on three blazing hooks that darted in under his hands. Red Schwartz was on deck, but Rockwell called on Belter Burke to pinch-hit. Belter was as tight as a drum and didn't have a chance. He, too, went down swinging.

That brought up Chip. The hurler was afraid of Chip and tried to keep them too tight. Chip dueled with him until it was a full count. The three-two pitch was a slider which ducked toward the outside corner. Chip went for it and golfed the ball over first for a clean single and the winning run was on first base. The fans were on their feet now, pleading with Butcher Durley to lace it out and break up the game.

Butcher crowded the plate, hunching his five-foot six-inch frame over the plate, challenging the chucker to drive him back. His daring was rewarded. The big lefty hooked them down low and close and got in a hole and then walked the husky little hot-corner guardian. Chip trotted down to second base.

Soapy had caught a beautiful game, working Byrnes as if they had been battery mates for years. And he had hit the ball. He advanced to the plate with grim determination. The visiting coach took a hand then, called time, and went into a huddle with the tall southpaw and the catcher. He must have known about Rock's pitching situation and that Byrnes was the only State pitcher who was available. Anyway, he decided to give Soapy a free ticket to get at Byrnes. Lefty had struck out three straight times. So they walked Soapy and that loaded the bases and put the problem squarely up to Rockwell.

The fans immediately set up a howl for a pinch hitter. You could hear them yelling for Nickels and Gillen and Emery and Burke—or just anyone who could hit!

"Get a hitter up there!"

"What's wrong with Nickels? He can hit!"

"How about Murph Gillen?"

Byrnes had been standing in the on-deck circle, hoping Soapy would clout one and dreading the responsibility of the situation. When he heard the crowd, he felt sure Rockwell would send in a pinch hitter. And he was relieved when the coach called time and advanced toward the plate. Then Lefty Byrnes got a shock. He could scarcely believe his ears.

"You can do it, Lefty," Rockwell said aggressively, patting him on the back. "Go on up there and win your own game!"

"Come on, Lefty," Chip yelled from his perch on third base. "Bring me in, buddy, bring me in!"

The crowd noise was earsplitting now and Byrnes was in something of a daze when he stepped into the batter's box. But he heard the yells of support from his teammates above the tumult of the crowd and above them all he could hear Chip Hilton. "Bring me in, Lefty! Bring me in!"

Lefty Byrnes was so befuddled by all the thoughts which were running through his mind that he never lifted the bat from his shoulder when the chucker whipped the first pitch across the plate. He was trying to convince himself that it was all true. "Imagine this,"

Lefty was thinking. "Rockwell tells me to win my own game and Chip Hilton calls me buddy."

Then it happened. Byrnes came out of his fog and leaned forward to pound his bat on the plate just as the Carleton chucker sidearmed a sharp hook high and on the inside and straight for Lefty's head.

Lefty saw the ball coming, all right, but he couldn't have moved to save his life. He had gone into a freeze and the speeding ball caught him smack in the middle of the forehead. Lefty toppled to the ground like a falling tree.

The crowd roar died as suddenly as a broadcast does when you snap off the radio. The game was forgotten. Only the umpire noted that Chip stepped on the plate when he stooped to help Rockwell lift Byrnes and carry him to the dugout. Indeed, only a few fans noted the tally on the scoreboard. And it wasn't until those few started to leave the stands that the crowd realized the game was over, that the bean ball which had stunned Lefty Byrnes had won the game for the Fence Busters.

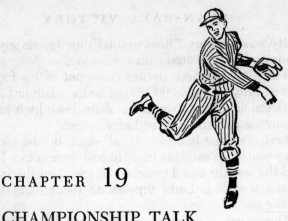

## CHAPTER 19

## CHAMPIONSHIP TALK

Doc Terring was out of the grandstand and down on the field before Rockwell and Chip and his teammates had carried Byrnes to the dugout, and almost as quickly, Byrnes was out of his stupor. He muttered something about a hit and struggled to get to his feet. Terring held him gently on the ground while he made a swift examination. When he finished, he looked up at Rockwell, relief showing on his face and his mouth twisted in a thankful smile.

"It isn't bad, Hank. Might have a slight concussion but nothing serious. We'll take him to the hospital for the night just to be sure. Jim Collins should be here any second now with his car."

"How about an X ray?" Rockwell queried.

"I don't need an X ray," Byrnes protested, struggling once more to gain his feet. "I'm all right! What happened?"

"You forgot to duck," Terring said gently.

"You mean I was beaned?" Byrnes demanded.

"That's right," Terring said, grinning. "But you won the game! Now, no more talking. Rock, get these kids away from here and help me get this boy to the hospital. Beat it now, you fellows. Here comes Collins with his car. Easy now, Byrnes."

"Can't we go along, Doc?" someone asked.

Terring shook his head. "Not now! You can visit him between eight and nine o'clock tonight."

Byrnes protested that he was all right, but Terring gave him little heed. He helped him gently but firmly into Collins' car and headed for the hospital. Rockwell went along. Chip and his teammates hurried away to get dressed, scarcely realizing they had won the game.

The irrepressible Soapy was well aware that they had gotten the jump on Carleton but he was subdued in his celebrating. He was holding back until he found out whether or not Byrnes was seriously hurt. Murph Gillen, Nickels, Emery, and Burke barged in shortly after nine o'clock, wearing broad smiles and bearing good news.

"He's O.K.," Gillen said happily. "No concussion, no nothing! No nothing except a headache!"

"That's right," Nickels added. "Doc Terring said he could come to the game tomorrow if there were no complications."

That was enough for Soapy. He hustled toward the storeroom to tell Chip. When he returned and took his place behind the fountain, he was his usual self and started right in to make up for lost time.

"You see, it was like this," Soapy said loudly, waving a spoon in the air and looking around until he had everyone's attention. "I get this hunch, see, so I goes to the Rockhead, that's the coach, you know, and I says 'Rock, ol' kid, if you got any ideas on winnin' this Carleton series, you better give a little thought to getting this here Lefty Byrnes back in uniform.'"

Soapy paused to make sure he had full control of the

situation and then continued in a confidential tone, leaning forward and speaking in a rasping whisper. "This Rock is a fair baseball coach, you know, but he isn't built for thinkin'. I've been takin' care of his inside baseball for years. Well, as I was sayin', I sells him on Byrnes—and, well, I guess you saw how the strategy worked. Not that I'm lookin' for any credit, of course. But wait! That isn't half of it.

"When Chip gets on and this Carleton sharpie fills the bases to set up a play at any base and get at Byrnes —the Rockhead is all for sendin' in a pinch hitter. But, just like always, I gets another hunch. 'Coach,' I says, 'remember you ain't got any more pitchers and besides I got a hunch this Byrnes is due!' Well, you know the rest and I don't want to pat myself on the back but—"

Soapy got patted right then! Fireball bopped him with an empty carton and everyone joined in a good-natured boo which brought Chip out of the storeroom to see what was happening. That started Soapy off again. He was still at it when they started home at eleven o'clock. Chip Hilton was happy and that was enough for Soapy Smith.

Lefty Byrnes had a lot of visitors that night. Jim Collins was there, proud as could be because of Lefty's victory. But deep inside he was most proud because Lefty had made such a great comeback. With himself, that is.

While Soapy was soapboxing, Chip got permission from George Grayson to make a short visit to the hospital. Byrnes was sitting up in bed, a bandage around his head, impatient and disgusted. But he grinned when Chip tiptoed into the room.

"I'm all right, Chip," he said quickly. "This is a lot of nonsense. I never felt better in my life!"

"I'm sure glad to hear that, Lefty. If we don't win tomorrow, I guess the coach will have to use you again on Monday. You really all right? I know what it means to get—"

Chip could have cut off his tongue. But it was too late. The words had been spoken. He looked wryly at Lefty, dismay filling his eyes.

Byrnes smiled understandingly. "That's all right, Chip. I've got it coming. Forget it!"

There was a long silence, each boy trying to think of some way to break the sudden tension which filled the room. Byrnes was the first to speak.

"Guess that's the opening I've been waiting for, Chip," he said haltingly. "You see, Chip, I know all about brushing back a batter. Too much, maybe—" Lefty paused, thinking back into the past. Then he continued, choosing his words carefully.

"A long time ago when I was playing sand-lot baseball, there was a fellow there who used to talk about pitching and the big leagues. I can see now that he just talked a good game. Anyway, he told me that good pitchers used the brush-back all the time, and if a batter wouldn't give ground, why you just threw one at his head and drove him out of there. He said that every big-league pitcher regarded the brush-back pitch as a privilege he was permitted as a pitching weapon."

"He was partly right, Lefty," Chip interrupted. "Gosh, a chucker wouldn't have a chance if the batter knew every pitch would be in the strike zone. Why, I don't know any pitcher who doesn't use a curve or some sort of sidearm pitch to fool the batter. Rock himself tells us to pitch tight to the good hitters. Of course he doesn't tell us to throw at their heads or try to hit them."

Byrnes nodded. "I know, Chip. But you see, this man I'm talking about told me that you could make any batter hit the dirt by throwing the ball *behind* his head."

"He was right about that, I guess," Chip said thoughtfully. "A fellow always ducks back when a ball is thrown at him. Or else he drops to the ground. So far as I'm concerned, I don't believe any pitcher deliberately throws at a batter's head. I guess you and I know how hard it is to find the strike zone at times. No matter how hard a guy tries, the ball gets away once in a while. No, I don't think any pitcher tries deliberately to hit a batter. It just doesn't make sense."

"That's right, Chip," Byrnes agreed soberly, lifting his hand to the bandage on his head. "But once in a while a fellow who doesn't know any better makes a mistake. I don't think the Carleton pitcher tried to hit me today. That's for sure. He wouldn't risk hitting me when it meant the loss of the game. But once in a while a pitcher makes a mistake even when it's not in a game."

There was an awkward silence and then Byrnes continued. "You see, Chip, what I'm trying to get at is— Well, the ball I threw at you, the one which hit you in the elbow— I tried to hit you with that ball, Chip."

Chip smiled and shook his head. "I don't believe it! You're not that kind of fellow and you could swear that on a stack of Bibles and I wouldn't believe it. O.K.?"

Byrnes tried to protest but Chip stopped him. "Listen, Lefty," Chip said earnestly, "that's all over. My arm is as good as new—or it will be in a couple of days. Let's forget all that stuff. It's not important now. The big thing is the series with Carleton and then the championship. It's a cinch. Now that we're all back together again. Right? See you tomorrow."

Chip reached the door before he remembered the chief purpose of his visit. He reached into his pocket and drew out a ball. It was the game ball which he had picked up beside the plate.

"Gosh, I nearly forgot. All the fellows thought you might like to have this, Lefty. It's the game ball. The one which cracked you on the head."

"You mean the bean ball," Lefty said, smiling. "Maybe we ought to call it the pumpkin ball. My head's about that empty. Thanks, Chip. Thanks a lot."

After Chip left, Byrnes turned the ball over and over in his hands. It was covered with names. The names of the Fence Busters. All of them! And the two names Lefty looked at the longest were Chip Hilton and Henry Rockwell.

Saturday afternoon the fans stormed the stands, wondering just who Rockwell would pull out of his hat this time, who he would send to the mound to win the all-important game. University fans were solidly behind the Fence Busters once again, solidly behind the Comeback Kids. And as they jammed into the grandstand and the bleachers, they were full of Little Four championship talk.

Lefty Byrnes was sitting in the dugout, watching the Carleton hitting practice and enjoying to the full his newly found feeling of peace. The victory had given him a tremendous lift. But there was something else which was most responsible, and every once in a while his eyes shifted to the figure of Chip Hilton who was leisurely playing catch with Murph Gillen in front of the bleachers. Lefty was in the midst of a lot of pleasant thoughts when Doc Terring sauntered up and joined Rockwell in front of the dugout. Byrnes listened to the conversation without thinking much about it at first. Then he began to strain his ears, to catch every word.

Rockwell greeted Terring morosely. "Hiya, Doc. Looks bad!"

"What looks bad?" Terring asked, grinning amiably.

Rockwell looked at him sharply. "You can see for yourself, can't you? I don't have a chucker."

"What about Maxim or Dean?"

Rockwell snorted impatiently. "Now isn't that a smart question! You know as well as I do that they're both nursing sore arms. Neither one could throw hard enough to break a pane of glass!"

"How about Smith?"

Rockwell snorted again. "You know he's not a pitcher. He wouldn't last through the first inning!"

"Well, frankly, I don't know what you're worrying about," Terring said lightly. "You've got the best pitcher in the country all ready and raring to go! I don't know why you don't use him."

"Isn't funny! Who?"

"Chip Hilton!"

"Chip? You mean his arm's all right?"

"It's perfect. Right now, I'd say he's faster than ever."

"But he hasn't been throwing. Really throwing, I mean."

"Oh, yes, he has! He's been throwing real hard. For two weeks!"

"Where? When?"

Terring snickered provokingly, delaying his answer, enjoying Rockwell's confusion to the fullest. "Behind my house," he said gleefully. "Chip's been throwing and I've been doing the receiving. Every evening for two straight weeks. And he's sharp. Real sharp!"

Rockwell's jaw squared and he threatened Terring with his fist. "Why, you—"

Terring chuckled and winked at Byrnes. "Another

thing, Rock. Chip's been ready for a week. You could have used him yesterday—if you had needed him!"

Lefty Byrnes clouted Belter Burke on the back and leaped out of the dugout. "Yippee," he shouted. "Yippee! Chip, you hear that? Hear that, Chip! Doc says you're O.K.!"

## CHAPTER 20

## TEAM NO-HITTER

CHIP smoothed the dirt in front of the rubber and then turned to walk back of the mound. As he swung around, he carried with him the picture of his receiver, good old dependable Soapy, thumping his glove and gazing at him with all the confidence a fellow could ever deserve.

Soapy Smith was a smart catcher with a strong, rapid-fire arm which sent the ball whizzing on a clothesline to any base. And he could hit! Who could ask for a better battery mate!

Chip's eyes flickered around the field, checking the rest of his teammates. Biggie Cohen, deep behind the base line, six-feet four-inches of first-class lefty first baseman. A great power hitter, fast afoot, strong throwing arm, two hundred and forty pounds of heart and all of it strong for his friends. One couldn't do better than that even in the big leagues. . . .

Hutch Kroll, squat, bowlegged, broad-shouldered keystone guardian, with big hands and lightning-fast legs. A holler guy who could back up what he had to say. Just the ticket for those lifesaving double plays. . . .

Speed Morris, long-time friend. Master of the long throw. An expert shortstop who could go deep into the hole and get them and peg them on a string. A dead-game fighter and as flashy in the field as a fellow could wish. . . .

Butcher Durley, strong, square-shouldered, hot-corner fighter. The Butcher fired them across the diamond like a shot from a rifle. He liked it when the going was tough, and played to win. . . .

Red Schwartz, home-town friend who never wavered in his loyalty on and off the field. Played with his heart every minute of every game. . . .

Fireball Finley, strictly a fullback. Big and rough and tough enough to bend the varsity line in the middle or off tackle. And fast enough to turn any end in the country. He could hit a ball a mile or chase a hit a mile. And get it. . . .

Murph Gillen, big and strong and fast. Good in the field and better than good with the willow. Filled with love of the game. A real competitor with guts enough to sit the bench and root for the fellow who had beat him out of a regular job. . . .

Out in the bull pen, Flash Sparks, Diz Dean, and Joe Maxim. An injury-stricken crew of chuckers who never quit and who rooted for you every time you faced a hitter. . . .

In the dugout, the fellows who had reported every day for practice and then had ridden the bench during the games. Leopoulos and Anderson and Roberts and McGuire. Real competitors. They knew what sports were all about. . . .

On the bench, a coach who never let you down. A

man who worked as hard as his players. A leader who played the game hard and straight and taught clean baseball. . . .

Last but not least, four great ballplayers sitting side by side in the dugout. Great fellows once they got straightened out. He could hear them chattering in the dugout, cheering the players on the field. Lefty Byrnes and Bob Emery and Belter Burke and Nick Nickels were part of the gang now.

A. & M. and Cathedral and Tech were in for a big surprise in the Little Four championship series. Now that the Fence Busters were intact again.

"Chip! What's the matter? The umpire's sore! He's yelled play ball three times!"

Chip hadn't heard a thing, but he reassured Soapy and told him he was ready. And even as he told his buddy everything was all right, Chip was thinking that he was the luckiest fellow in the world.

Carleton meant business. The lead-off man hit from the third-base side of the plate. Crowding for every inch, he was determined to start it off right. He was short and broad and had good eyes. Chip figured this hitter made you groove it before he flickered an eyelash. Chip teased him with a fast one, low outside, and the little guy never moved a muscle. A slider inside around the belt got the same treatment. Chip hooked the two-and-no pitch around the knees and the resounding crack which followed meant that the hitter had laid all the good wood on the ball. That meant distance!

Chip didn't look right away, and that's the reason he didn't see Finley take off without a backward glance and make a backhand stab at the ball. But he did look up in time to see Fireball haul it in and toss the ball to Schwartz. The crowd roar stilled the little shout he gave but he stood there until Fireball gave him the high sign.

"*Hmmmmm* . . . that was close," Chip murmured to himself.

The push-along hitter rapped Chip's first pitch right back at the mound. It was a high bouncer, a sure hit through the middle, had not Chip leaped high in the air at precisely the right instant to spear the ball. He threw the runner out at first and breathed another sigh of relief. But he was worried. Four pitches and two hard blows that had all the earmarks of sure hits but for two lucky stabs.

Chip took a long time before he looked for Soapy's sign. It was the first time in a long while that his confidence had been shaken. Maybe the layoff had done something to his arm. What if Doc Terring was wrong?

Soapy must have known what Chip was thinking, for he called time and came striding out along the alley. "You O.K., Chipper? Your arm all right?" he asked anxiously.

"Don't know, Soapy. Feels all right, but those two balls were hit hard."

"Purely coincidental," Soapy said vigorously. "Musta had their eyes closed. C'mon, throw it in! You got lots of help!"

Chip threw it in and he got the help. Not only that inning but through those which followed. And he needed all the help and all the breaks he could get, for the Carleton chucker was with it! Tall, wiry, and determined, he had blinding speed. He was wild enough to keep the hitters off balance but had enough control to keep out of trouble. Not that the Fence Busters didn't get to him, but they couldn't put their hits and their breaks together.

Going into the top of the fifth, Chip suddenly realized that he hadn't given up a hit and was building up to the magic one. For some time he had noted the change in the crowd, but it wasn't until he glanced out toward Fireball in center field and saw the goose eggs on the scoreboard that he realized where he was headed. He didn't feel too good about it, because Carleton runners had been on base almost every inning. He would have been in trouble time after time had it not been for the miraculous fielding of his teammates.

In the bottom of the eighth, with two long rows of goose eggs decorating the scoreboard, Durley led off with Gillen on deck and Soapy in the hole. Butcher hit from the third-base side of the plate and was a dangerous sticker. The third-base battler stood only five-six, but he was powerful and possessed a good eye. The Carleton pitcher fenced with Durley until the count was two and two and then broke the Butcher's back on a sharp-breaking curve for the third strike.

That brought up Murph Gillen. Gillen hit lefty and was a power hitter. But Murph wasn't thinking about the fences. He wanted desperately to get on base for a number of reasons. He would have taken a bean ball with a laugh if it meant he could reach first. He was ice up there. He waited them out until it was three and two and then blasted the ball over the second baseman's head and through right center clear to the fence. And he never stopped until he was perched on third.

That blow tore down the stands and brought the Carleton coach out to the mound. Soapy took a long time selecting a bat, his freckled face set with grim determination. But when he started up to the plate, Rockwell bounded out of the dugout and checked him.

"Hold it, Soapy," Rockwell said softly, grasping the

boy by the arm. "I've got to do something important right here. Sorry, kid, real sorry." He turned to the dugout. "Nickels!" he called sharply. "Hit for Smith!"

Nick nearly jumped out of his skin, and he moved like a streak getting out to the bat rack. He moved as if he was afraid Rockwell would change his mind. Nick had been doing a lot of thinking in the dugout. The big receiver was no fool and he realized that there was more to this than a pinch hitter. Smith had hit two for three and was catching a great game. Besides, Soapy had caught Chip Hilton for years and knew every move the chucker made. As he fumbled with the bats, Nick's thoughts nearly floored him. "Oh, what a chump I've been," he muttered. "If I can only—"

Everybody in the park was trying to figure the play. Bottom of the eighth, no score, one down, man on third. Good pitcher working, good hitter at the plate. Would Rockwell squeeze or hit? Nickels didn't look much like a push-along guy. The big fellow weighed two hundred and thirty pounds and was as tough as pig iron!

Jim Collins was one of those in the stands who was figuring. Beside him sat his pretty daughter Cindy. Her lovely eyes were on the outfielders. Jim always figured out loud at a ball game and today he was surrounded by a big circle of friends and fans. They were listening, too. Collins had called everything right so far.

Collins was emphatic. "He'll lay it down, squeeze in the run! He's got to! With Hilton pitching like a million bucks he can't afford to do anything else. Why, one run's as good as ten, the way the kid's going!"

The Carleton infield closed in, base-line distance, poised for the play at the plate, a bunt or a hit. The chucker kept them high and low, nothing good, and the count went to two and one, two balls and a called strike. Then, on the two-and-two pitch, Nick laid it down the third-base line just as if he had been doing that all his life.

"Wha'd I tell you!" Collins exploded. "Wha'd I tell you!"

Cindy Collins put her left hand under Jim's arm.

The Carley hot-corner guardian was in like a shot, set for the play at home. But he didn't have a chance. Gillen went in like a madman. He drove through the Carleton receiver as though he wasn't there and spread-eagled on the plate as if he meant to pin it to the clay for three minutes. The Carleton third baseman cast a rueful glance at the plate and threw to first, getting Nick by ten feet. But it didn't matter right then, not to the fans. They were stomping and cheering, and Gillen was mobbed by his teammates all the way to the dug-out. That brought Chip up and he tried to add to the insurance. But the best he could do was a long, high fly which carried to the right-center fence. The center fielder pulled it in and that was that!

Baseball fans are in a class by themselves. What other group could or would keep their fingers crossed when a fellow was fashioning a record? Beyond that, what group would refrain from cheering the hero on? Not many! This crowd was different.

Perhaps amateur baseball fans are in a different class from the experts who mastermind the pros in the big parks. At any rate, the fans who were gathered in Alumni Field that Saturday afternoon had been pulling with all their hearts for the tall, blond chucker who had been the victim of so many tough breaks during the season. "Why, the kid's been playin' with one arm all banged up!"

Chip walked out slowly for the top of the ninth with

a million thoughts flooding his mind, each trying to get the most attention. Three outs! Three hitters and the Rock would have a chance at the Little Four championship. And Soapy and Biggie and Speed and Red and Fireball and all the gang would get the reward they deserved for fighting so hard and doggedly through the season.

Nickels' face was grim and every return of the warm-up pitches to the mound expressed the pent-up determination he felt. The rest were all the same.

In the dugout, Lefty Byrnes was throwing every ball with Chip. The happy chucker had pulled an about-face in every way. He and Emery and Burke pulled and swayed every time a pitch missed the strike zone. The Fence Busters were a team again. On the field and on the bench.

The tough little lead-off man who had caused so much trouble all through the game was up there again. And he got the jump on Chip. He worked the count to three and two. Nickels called for the hook but Chip shook him off. The little guy had tagged two of those!

Nick then called for the slider and Chip gave it all he had. The ball headed for the outside corner and broke across the plate right under the wrists. The Carley hit it all right, but on the handle of the bat, and the ball went spinning crazily down the first-base line.

Biggie swooped in on the ball like a big cat and pivoted around just in time to avoid the charging runner. Without pausing, it seemed, Biggie drilled the ball like a flash of light straight into Hutch Kroll's eager mitt. Hutch couldn't have dropped the ball if he had tried. In fact, he put on a pantomime, pretending he had to pry each of his glove fingers off the ball one at a time.

The fans ate that up. It was a partial release from the excitement which kept mounting and mounting inside their chests and which they had been trying to hold.

The push-along hitter, batting from the third-base side of the plate had hit the ball hard, twice in a row, right up the middle. Chip had fielded the first one, but the second had streaked past him on the third-base side of the rubber and was on its way until Speed Morris had come from nowhere, it seemed, to pick up the ball on the dead run back of second base. The speedster had pivoted in the air and thrown a perfect strike to Cohen to nip the runner by a whisker. That brought down the house and was just a sample of the kind of support Chip had been receiving.

Chip, trying to keep the ball in close to the hitter, got behind two and no. A sharp hook caught the outside corner for a called strike and then Chip came back with the fast one. The batter met it right on the nose and the ball didn't rise three feet from the ground. It headed straight for the Butcher and nearly bowled him over but he held it. That made it two away.

And now, Chip and the Fence Busters were one out away from the championship series. Henry Rockwell was sitting deep in the dugout, leaning forward, hands supporting his chin, living through one of those priceless high-premium moments a coach dreams about. Rock's eyes were fixed on Chip, all his hopes pinned on the slender youngster's arm.

The batter was the Carleton center fielder. Hitting lefty, the big fellow had struck out twice and hit one clear to the right-center fence. Fireball had practically climbed the fence to spear that one. Chip worked the count to one and two and then tried to slip in a curve. He slipped it in all right, but the batter pivoted and met the ball with the fat part of the bat, pulling a low-rising line drive over first.

Chip had finished in his fielding position, feet spread, arms hanging loose, ready for a play. And he stayed right there, turning only his head to see Biggie leap high in the air in a futile effort to reach the ball.

Murph Gillen was an even six feet in height and weighed two hundred and ten pounds, but one would never have known it. Judging, that is, by the sprinter's start he made as he drove toward the ball. Gillen had shifted a bit to his left out in right field but he was far away from the drive. The ball was far ahead and far to his left.

Chip wanted to close his eyes but something held them fast. Just when it seemed that the ball had dipped to hit the ground he saw Gillen dive. Gillen dove for the ball and went head over heels and up on his feet with the precious sphere clutched tightly in both hands.

The first-base umpire was right on the play and Biggie was right behind him. And when the umpire's thumb went up over his head, Biggie grasped Gillen in his powerful arms and lifted him high in the air, shouting over and over, "What a play! What a play!"

When Biggie put Gillen down they were too happy to hear the booming shouts and continuous roar which followed the umpire's gesture. Then Gillen sobered and he said something which was a lot more important to Biggie than the grandstand catch.

"That one was for Chip," Gillen said grimly. "For Chip and the team and Rock—"

Gillen never finished that sentence because Biggie had him up in the air again, and then they were surrounded by Soapy and Nick and Speed and all the gang. And when Byrnes and Emery and Burke arrived they grabbed Chip and up he went beside Gillen. Then Rockwell and Terring and Jim Collins came rushing up to join in the celebration and that made it complete. The Fence Busters were indeed a team again.

Chip and Murph were trying to scramble down from the shoulders of that happy gang but it was no use. So they substituted a "put-and-take" contest instead, as each tried to force the game ball into the hands of the other.